SUDDEN FLASH YOUTH

Other Persea Anthologies

IMAGINING AMERICA
Stories from the Promised Land
Edited by Wesley Brown and Amy Ling

AMERICA STREET
A Multicultural Anthology of Stories
Edited by Anne Mazer

GOING WHERE I'M COMING FROM
Memoirs of American Youth
Edited by Anne Mazer

WORKING DAYS
Short Stories About Teenagers at Work
Edited by Anne Mazer

STARTING WITH "I"
Personal Essays by Teenagers
Youth Communication
Edited by Andrea Estepa and Philip Kay

VIRTUALLY NOW
Stories of Science, Technology, and the Future
Edited by Jeanne Schinto

BIG CITY COOL
Short Stories About Urban Youth
Edited by M. Jerry Weiss and Helen S. Weiss

FISHING FOR CHICKENS
Short Stories About Rural Youth
Edited by Jim Heynen

OUTSIDE RULES
Short Stories About Nonconformist Youth
Edited by Claire Robson

SUDDEN FLASH YOUTH

65 Short-Short Stories

EDITED BY

Christine Perkins-Hazuka,

Tom Hazuka, and Mark Budman

A Karen and Michael Braziller Book

PERSEA BOOKS / NEW YORK

Persea Books, Inc.
277 Broadway
New York, New York 10007

Library of Congress Cataloging-in-Publication Data
Sudden flash youth : 65 short-short stories / edited by Christine Perkins-
Hazuka, Tom Hazuka, and Mark Budman. – 1st ed.
       p. cm.
ISBN 978-0-89255-371-6 (alk. paper)
1. Short stories, American. I. Perkins-Hazuka, Christine. II. Hazuka, Tom. III.
Budman, Mark.
PS648.S5S84 2011
813.008'035235—dc23

                    011021284

Designed by Rita Lascaro
Manufactured in the United States of America
First Edition

Contents

Editors' Note

Since the appearance of the pioneering anthologies *Sudden Fiction* (1986) and *Flash Fiction* (1992), the world of sudden/flash fiction has expanded exponentially. These stories were an immediate hit with readers, writers, and editors alike, and today numerous short-short story anthologies exist, in addition to many literary magazines (both print and online) dedicated to the form. But no sudden/flash fiction anthology has concentrated on youth, our formative years of choices and challenges. The stories in *Sudden Flash Youth* feature protagonists under the age of twenty, with an exclusive focus on childhood and adolescent situations—in other words, the myriad experiences of growing up.

Growing up in America is an incredibly wide-ranging topic, and we have selected stories that cover as many varieties of that experience as we could find. Literary excellence was always the main criterion, but once a story passed the quality test we tried to craft a collection of fiction that reflected as broad a swath of America as possible. Few people who open *Sudden Flash Youth* know what it's like to be eighty years old, but every one of the book's readers has been a child and a teenager. We share a wide, deep pool of experiences, whether those events occurred last week or fifty years ago, in suburban New England or the rural South, at the Canadian border or somewhere on the endless highways of the West. Reading these stories of youth we inevitably recall and compare our own memories, and vicariously expand our lives.

Though short, these stories don't lack substance. Though about youth, they don't lack universal appeal. Though literary, they don't lack action. They examine love, faith, sports, death, accidents, toys, pets, even the end of the world. Some pieces refer to historical events: slavery, segregation, life in the 1950s, and the Korean and Vietnam wars.

In Katharine Weber's "Sleeping," a story reminiscent of Chekhov in its combination of gentle sadness and intensity, a young girl's evening of babysitting opens mysteries she will never forget. In L.C. Fiore's "No Wake Zone," the son of Iranian immigrants faces the daunting next step in his life while weighed down by his parents' foreign, unknowable past. In Dave Eggers' "Accident," the threat of violence hangs in the air when the protagonist causes an accident to a car full of teenagers. It's the only story in this book with an adult protagonist, but it uniquely reveals how mistrust of the "other" can be overcome by the healing power of empathy.

Sudden Flash Youth also includes stories by lesser-known writers who deserve a wider audience, including several whose fiction is published here for the first time. In "Half Sleep," by Matt Krampitz, the interaction between a boy and his beloved older brother, now a junkie and teenage thief, propels the story to an unexpected climax. Kathleen O'Donnell's "First Virtual" combines the age-old issue of a girl pressured to have sex, with contemporary concerns about technology and the nature of reality. David Partenheimer's "Pep Assembly at Evergreen Junior High" uses a wry, ironic voice to put a fresh spin on the conflicts of peer pressure and bullying in school.

Whether the story is as funny as Ron Carlson's "Homeschool Insider: The Fighting Pterodactyls" or as devastating as Alice Walker's "The Flowers," we hope that readers of all ages find within the pages of *Sudden Flash Youth* something valuable, entertaining, and educational, something as fresh as youth itself. These stories do not take long to read, yet like the experiences of childhood they will stay with the reader for a long time after.

A final word is in order about the length of these stories. Curiously, specific definitions of sudden fiction and flash fiction remain elusive. *Flash Fiction* used a 750-word limit for its stories. Some editors expand their definition of flash fiction to 1,000 words; others contract it to 500. *Sudden Fiction* had a 2,000-word maximum. In *Sudden Flash Youth* we have created a hybrid in both title and length, welcoming stories of up to 1,000 words, although most are considerably shorter. But who's counting? Readers just want good stories, so please feel free to turn the page and enter youthful worlds that are common to all of us, different for each of us, and gone in a sudden flash.

Christine Perkins-Hazuka
Tom Hazuka
Mark Budman

SUDDEN FLASH YOUTH

Tamazunchale

ROBERT SHAPARD

The highway had turned tropical and potholed, two narrow lanes and narrower bridges, with butterflies spattering the grill-screen we bought on good advice at the border.

My mother said, "We're on the wrong road." The map was flapping, and her hair, still blond then, was flaying, air thudding through the open windows of the Buick. "We're lost."

My father sang "On the Road to Mandalay." Years later, my mother said he was sometimes a stranger, after the war, although he never seemed strange to me. He had been in combat both in Europe and the Pacific, but he rarely spoke of it. He worked for an oil company, and we moved often. I was only ten at the time of our vacation, and he died when I was sixteen.

The small patch of tropics, which was not shown on my mother's map but through which we had been traveling, soon thinned out as we climbed into the desert mountains. We followed a big, backfiring diesel that we couldn't pass. I lay in the backseat drowsing in the heat and the swaying and could tell from the backfires when the diesel was speeding downhill, leaving us farther behind, and when it was laboring uphill, slowing, making us draw closer again. My father spoke enthusiastically about the great city we were going to—Mexico City, high above everything, ancient and beautiful. Nothing ever changed there. My mother, so practical, consulted guidebooks by the dozen and wrote itineraries. I remember mostly rain and traffic jams.

It was hot and growing dusky when a village appeared below us. Later we found it on the map: Tamazunchale, which my mother pronounced "Thomas 'n' Charlie." It was a few whitewashed houses in a dusty bend, treetops shining in the late sun. Ahead of us the diesel was plummeting toward a one-lane bridge, and around the curve on the other side of the village, a small green pickup suddenly appeared, flashing its headlights. But the diesel barreled onto the bridge at top speed, not trying to slow at all, so that the pickup, in order to avoid disaster, was forced into a skid on the village side. It flipped and rolled, and as the diesel shot past, the pickup slammed finally onto its side in a wave of dust and gravel.

"God, oh God." We followed slowly downhill in the Buick. When we crossed the bridge, the dust swallowed us. Then, as it cleared, we saw the underside of the pickup. Some villagers had already reached it. Others were still running: village women with their skirts clutched up, crying. There was a strong smell of Pemex gasoline, and around one of the tires was a pale flame. One of the men, wearing white campesino pants but bare-chested, stretched down into the skyward window, while others held his ankles. He fetched up a howling infant.

"We've got to stop," my mother said.

Probably there was a farm family in the pickup, which had pink and green tassels and curtains painted on the inside of the windshield, a decoration common to many Mexican trucks. We had slowed almost to a stop, but not entirely. We were going on.

"They need help," my mother said.

"They've got help," my father said.

"We could take them to a hospital," my mother said.

"They'll call for help," my father said.

I watched, through the rear window, the villagers crowding around. There were streaks of black in the dust cloud, but never an explosion. The cloud billowed, huge and serene.

"But what if there's no telephone?" my mother said. "How will they call for help?"

The diesel must have continued up the mountain. It had not stopped to render aid. It was nowhere in sight.

"You don't know what could happen," my father said. "You don't understand, do you?"

My mother was not a hysterical woman. If there were shouts and tears I don't remember them. If she had doubts, as she always did, about everything in her life, she took refuge in my father's direction. She never remarried.

"They'll think it's our fault," she said reasonably. "They'll come after us. They'll throw us in jail."

My father began to sing "On the Road to Mandalay."

My mother's map flapped furiously. Later she gave him some water from the cap of the big thermos she kept at her feet. When we traveled nights, there were always the embers of the cigarettes they passed between them.

I watched all the way to the top of the mountain. In the evening light, rising above the village, the dust was like a pink bomb blast: a great, unfolding flower. I understood only that my mother and father were lost.

Chalk

MEG KEARNEY

It was my idea. Yellow chalk on red brick, just above the water fountain. *Write it big,* whispered Margaret, as if it weren't Sunday afternoon and we weren't the only kids hanging on school property. Fat yellow letters on red brick. The first to see it would be the walkers who cut across the basketball court just before the Monday morning bell. Next would come first-period gym, then word would spread like blood on a white skirt: CHERYL DUKE GOES BOTH WAYS. I didn't know exactly what that meant, "both ways," but when my brother John said it he sounded like he did when he talked about Delmore Spitz, the mean jealous jerk who'd keyed John's shiny new used truck from the driver's door all the way to the tailgate. So whatever it meant, it must be bad, I thought, rushing through the last "S." I felt kind of queasy all of a sudden, but I laughed it off with Margaret as we tore across the court toward home.

I'd run across that court countless more times with Margaret than I had with William, but he and I had spent our share of time there playing Pig and Horse and one-on-one. None of his other friends called him William, just me. I wrote his name again and again in my notebook, making the letters tall and lanky the way his body is. I like the way those vertical letters look like timber, like a stand of trees. That miniature forest of his name felt strong and safe and loving, like him.

And now he was with her. Cheryl called him Bill, like everybody else. She didn't know shit about him. I really didn't know shit about her, either, as she was new since September. One of those Catholic school kids who transferred after eighth grade. Margaret said Cheryl could suck chrome off a fender, but Margaret said that about anyone who stole another girl's boyfriend.

Margaret shut the door to my room as I slid the chalk in my backpack, then dug it out again and ditched it in the garbage can under my desk. I wanted to ask her if she knew what "goes both ways" really meant. She was a year older and prided herself on being more advanced about stuff like that. But she was already on my bed flipping through my poetry books so I didn't say a thing. I stared at the yellow dust on my hands and thought of Delmore Spitz. Mean jealous jerk. Why was I thinking of him again? He was a schmuck, my grandmother would have said—the kind of guy who sweet-talks you all the way to third base and then never calls you again.

I wiped chalk dust on my jeans, then regretted it. William and I were covered in chalk dust after a game of Love & War. It was a game we'd made up. One basketball was "Love" and the other was "War." When the scoring got too complicated we tracked it in chalk on the blacktop just outside the key. Soon we were keeping score on each other, strokes of chalky sun across our Mountain Jam T-shirts, blazes down our blue jeans. By the time we quit, we were bright as beach balls. Even his kisses tasted like chalk, but I didn't mind.

Yellow chalk on red brick. I might as well have signed my name underneath. Cheryl probably wouldn't know who did it, but William would. And now it was nearly dark—too late to run back and try to erase it or scratch it out. William would know. I could try to get to school super early, before anyone else—but the maintenance men were there at the crack of dawn. I'd be caught yellow-handed. I lay down on the bed, knowing already I'd be too sick to go to school in the morning.

Margaret said later that the sound I'd made when I lay down was like a dog who'd got his tail run over by a car. Not like a girl, she stressed, but a wounded animal. When nothing she'd said made me feel better, she left me there like that. On her way out she told my mom in the kitchen that she thought I was sick, and Mom came in and felt my forehead and pulled the afghan over me. I just curled up like a baby. Like a mean jealous jerk of a baby. Like the baby schmuck that I was. Soon William would know I was, too.

I didn't set the alarm and Mom didn't bother to wake me before she'd gone to work. What shook me out of bed was the banging at my window. I thought he'd break the glass—I thought his fist would come clear through. William! I cried, pulling on a sweatshirt. But it was a girl's voice that answered. A girl screaming everything that I already knew was true.

Twins

PAMELA PAINTER

Our house is hopping when I get in from Little League. The Hennesseys, Cardulos, people up and down the street are sitting on the porch with no drinks and the dog is going apeshit in the basement. Dad says the Vinales were in an accident. Mrs. Vinales is still under observation, but doing well considering. Mr. Vinale's leg has already been operated on. Vinny, the twin with the missing front tooth is being "prepared"—Mrs. Hennessey's word—at Spassky's Funeral home across town. Dad's hand rests heavy on my shoulder when he tells me Bobby, the other twin, is in my bedroom. We're waiting for his uncle from Toledo to take him home. He says Bobby asked to play my drums. I picture busted snares, splintered drumsticks and double time the stairs.

My door is closed and Mom is singing Bobby "The Little Brown Fox" even though our whole family knows his favorite word is *screw.* Saturday nights I babysit the twins. To find out which is which, I tickle them. Vinny has the missing front tooth; Bobby's grin is all white and sharp. I dig my fingers into their ribs till they howl.

Bobby is poking my drumsticks into his snotty nose. I sit at the bottom of the bed where his feet can't reach me. Mom gives me the eye—like I'll know what to say. When she leaves, I tap Bobby's shoes as if I'm playing the drums. We both start to sniffle. I tell him it's okay. I promise him no tickling ever again. I tell him he won't even have to smile.

First Virtual

KATHLEEN O'DONNELL

Everyone always comments on how perfect we are for each other. How we're always laughing and finishing each other's sentences. That it seems like we've always been together.

I'm not into looks or anything, but Blue is perfect in that respect, too: he's impossibly tall, with muscle upon muscle and inky black hair that falls dramatically over his forehead. I love to push it back with my fingers, because then he always catches my hands in his and doesn't let go.

Blue and I haven't said the word yet, but I'm sure we will soon. We're almost saying it. My mom's worried we're going too fast, but we can't help it. We almost did it last night, but I stopped him just in time. I know he was upset, but I had to. I wanted to be sure that he really cared.

Because he's my first virtual.

My friend Jen says virtual doesn't hurt, but what does she know? She's had real and virtual boyfriends. I'm sixteen and Blue is my first boyfriend and my first virtual both, which makes it even more important that our first time means something. If he laughs, or worse, disappears, I'll die.

Last night, after I stopped him pulling off my clothes in the cottage we'd built in *betterlife,* the local teen portal where we'd met, there was an expression on his avatar's face he'd never put there before. It was angry and dismissive, as if he was looking through me. A look I have a lot of practice with in real life. I'm not hideous or anything, I'm just nothing special:

brown hair, brown eyes, resolutely average. That's why I made sure to make my avatar tall and flame-haired and extra curvy.

Tonight, after I log in, Blue doesn't answer when I knock on our door, but I know he's home. There's a light on in the attic where he likes to play guitar and I can hear soft chords coming out of the window.

"C'mon, Blue," I say. "I'm sorry. I just got scared. You know I—" I falter for a second, then have my avatar take a deep breath and blurt it out, "I love you, Blue, okay?"

The strumming stops and Blue opens the door. The look he wears now is my favorite: eyes shining, his smile taking over his whole face. He pulls me onto our bed and starts to unbutton my sweater, then stops when I pull away. "What's the problem, Red? I thought you said you loved me."

"I do," I insist. There's a strong breeze coming through the window—he's tried that trick before, it was how he first got me under the covers with him—but I stay on my side of the bed. "I do love you. But I'm not ready yet." I have my avatar take his hand and stroke his fingers and he tightens them around mine.

"If you love me," he says, staring straight into my eyes, with the melting look that kills me—I helped him design it and he knows just when to use it—"then prove it."

I start to shake. "I said I love you, Blue. But can't we wait a little? Please?"

"C'mon, Red. What're you worried about?" His voice is soft and gentle. "You can't get in trouble here. C'mon. I'm not gonna hurt you." But when I don't move, his face hardens. "Okay, okay. We don't have to do it tonight. We can do something else, something even better."

I'm so relieved I agree instantly, my avatar relaxing into his without hearing what he wants. Now his hands are shaking and he's the one to pull away.

"You'll do it?" he asks, his voice breaking a little. "You'll really do it? Oh, God, Red, I love you, too. You know I do. And I'll still love you after."

"After?" I'm trying not to shake again, but my hands are trembling so hard on the keyboard my avatar starts back up.

"After we meet for real." Blue cups my face tightly in his hands and won't let go. "No avatars. No software. Just us."

For three days, I stay logged out of *betterlife*. I know Blue will use his tender look and his coaxing voice, and I'll give in.

When I can't stand missing him anymore, I play the file I saved, of when he first touched my hair. It made me shiver then, and it makes me shiver now. What would it be like to know him and touch him for real? Would his skin be as warm as I imagined? Would his kisses still be so wild and intense? Would he still love me?

After four days, I break down at lunch and ask Jen what I should do. "Meet him or don't. What's the big deal?" she asks, then points at my fries. "You done with those?"

That night, I log in and tell Blue I miss him and I love him but I can't meet him. He hates it when I make my avatar cry, he thinks it's cheating, but I'm not, I'm crying for real, wiping my tears with my non-keyboard hand. I tell him I can't lose him but I'll do anything he wants, as long as we stay together in *betterlife*.

Jen was wrong. Virtual did hurt.

He was brutal and quick and he didn't say he loved me. He didn't say anything at all. Afterward, he forgot to hold me and when he finally spoke, he said he had somewhere to be.

* * *

I wait in *betterlife* every night, but Blue never comes back. His guitar's gone and he's deleted all our history. I guess he would've deleted our cottage too, if I hadn't locked the design. But that's not the worst.

The worst is that Blue was wrong, too. Trouble does happen in *betterlife*. And my avatar's period is four weeks late.

Heartland

DAPHNE BEAL

The person who I am, um, sleeping with (sorry, Mom, sorry, Dad), which I say because we are not allowed to say "dating" or "boyfriend" or "girlfriend," or any of those other clichés, because we, *he*, is very interested in inhabiting a particular transcendent, non-pedestrian state. This person—whose name I can't tell you, and who, yes, does have a few gray hairs—holds my hand, his slender fingers interlaced with mine next to a ginger ale we are sharing on a plane from NYC to New Orleans (where no one knows I am except my best friend at school). He is telling me the place I come from doesn't exist. He's not talking about the small, too cutely named city in central Wisconsin where I grew up —he's not that kind of mystic—he's talking about the Midwest.

"Amanda," says my older man, which he calls me and I accept, because he's right: Mandy does sound like a doll's name. "It's a fictional construct, a myth of convenience."

I look at him, the filmmaker I am *shtupping*—a Yiddishism I come by honestly despite my Protestant roots, because dear So-and-So is Jewish—and part of me wants to agree. I love the movie he made in Kansas (where he lived as a kid), complete with nods to Toto and friends. Still, it rankles me, him telling me where I am from, or not from, as if he simply knows better.

"But that makes no sense," I say, thinking, *I am up for this*. Fresh from two midterm papers this past week, my synapses are primed. "If the myths are abiding and in wide circulation—" a B+, at least, "the Midwest exists as much as any place with an identity attached to it does. It's like saying there's no America." He raises an eyebrow. "Okay," I say, "no such thing as the South."

He looks at me with a familiar half-smile and says, "No geographical borders, no wars fought over it, and do you really think going to a mall in Lacrosse is all that different from going to one in Schenectady?" I free my hand from his and put it between my legs, because my fingers are cold, always cold.

"Never mind," I say.

"Amanda, it's just an idea."

Resting my forehead on the plastic window, I feel suddenly weary of being this person's portable, cantankerous muse, his juicy little piece, whatever. I imagine crawling out on the wing and dropping into the layers of clouds below—cotton candy, cotton batting, a land of fluff 'n' stuff—and rolling around like I've wanted to since I was a kid.

In New Orleans, the air has body it's so thick. It's only March, but as we ride from the airport past houses that look like someone's taken a baseball bat to them, trees burst with white and pink blossoms, unabashed, and strange beauty is everywhere.

So-and-So slides across the lumpy seat, places his palm on my cheek. "Hey, let's have a good time, okay?" I lean into him, tucking my irritation away like a stone in my pocket.

That afternoon, we walk the gravel-lined path on Esplanade down to the river, where we eat beignets and drink coffee, and take a ferry back and forth across the slow-churning Mississippi.

On his friend Josie's porch in the dark, he and I sit in rockers, and she tells my guy, "I've never seen you so happy," as she pushes herself back and forth on the swing. Her husband, Gary, rests his leonine head in her lap and places his big feet on the side of the house. Later that night, in the loft bed in their office, So-and-So tells me Gary is cheating on Josie.

"I think it's lousy," he says. "But I also think she's kind of a fool to stay with him." Sometimes, it's not clear to me whether So-and-So likes women, or girls, whatever category you want to put me in. He loves them—us—but I suspect he thinks we are all a little bit dumb and, maybe, secretly cruel.

We go to hear music at a place where someone was shot outside the week before. We ride the trolley up St. Charles, eat oysters, drink beer. But the thing I like best is that no one looks at us curiously here, the way they do everywhere else.

Then, on the last morning, we walk to the park where Gary and Josie were married the year before and sit beside a pond, under what I've learned is a magnolia, surrounded by goose shit.

"I slept with someone," I tell him.

"I knew it," he says, popping up. He kicks at a rock embedded in the shiny dirt and looks back at me. "Is he better than me?"

"I'm not talking about it. I'm just telling you it happened." I am not about to describe the water-polo player, with his nice shoulders and goofy smile, who, instead of asking me in the middle of the night, "Do you *want* me to fall in love with you, Amanda?" grabs me by the waist and says, "God, you're hot!"

So-and-So, dry-eyed and demoralized, says, "Well, we can't just sit here."

At Josie's, he calls me a cab (I'm going alone now), and I take a picture of us, not sure if there will be another. The drizzle turns to rain as the car pulls away, and the rivulets snaking down the glass make the window feel like a mirror.

The driver turns to examine me. "What's the matter, honey?" he says. "Did he want to marry you?"

"No," I say, grateful that anyone cares.

"Well, whatever it is, you don't have to worry too much," he says. "You're still so young." In the days and weeks and months to come, I make myself repeat what I've been told, *I am young, I am young, I am young.*

Confession

STUART DYBEK

Father Boguslaw was the priest I waited for, the one whose breath through the thin partition of the confessional reminded me of the ventilator behind Vic's Tap. He huffed and smacked as if in response to my dull litany of sins, and I pictured him slouched in his cubicle draped in vestments, the way he sat slumped in the back entrance to the sacristy before saying morning mass—hung over, sucking an unlit Pall Mall, exhaling smoke.

Once, his head thudded against the wooden box.

"Father," I whispered, "Father," but he was out, snoring. I knelt, wondering what to do, until he finally groaned and hacked himself awake.

As usual, I'd saved the deadly sins for last: the lies and copied homework, snitching drinks, ditching school, and hitchhiking, which I'd been convinced was an offense against the Fifth Commandment, prohibiting suicide. Before I reached the dirty snapshots of Korean girls, stolen from the dresser of my war hero uncle, Uncle Al, and still unrepentantly cached behind the oil shed, he knocked and said I was forgiven.

As for Penance: "Go in peace, my son, I'm suffering enough today for both of us."

Sleeping

KATHARINE WEBER

She would not have to change a diaper, they said. In fact, she would not have to do anything at all. Mrs. Winter said that Charles would not wake while she and Mr. Winter were out at the movies. He was a very sound sleeper, she said. No need to have a bottle for him or anything. Before the Winters left they said absolutely please don't look in on the sleeping baby because the door squeaked too loudly.

Harriet had never held a baby, except for one brief moment, when she was about six, when Mrs. Antler next door had surprisingly bestowed on her the tight little bundle that was their new baby, Andrea. Harriet had sat very still and her arms had begun to ache from the tension by the time Mrs. Antler took back her baby. Andy was now a plump seven-year-old, older than Harriet had been when she held her that day.

After two hours of reading all of the boring mail piled neatly on a desk in the bedroom and looking through a depressing wedding album filled with photographs of dressed-up people in desperate need of orthodonture (Harriet had just ended two years in braces and was very conscious of malocclusion issues) while flipping channels on their television, Harriet turned the knob on the baby's door very tentatively, but it seemed locked. She didn't dare turn the knob with more pressure because what if she made a noise and woke him and he started to cry?

She stood outside the door and tried to hear the sound of a baby breathing, but she couldn't hear anything through the door except the sound of the occasional car that passed by on the street outside. She wondered what Charles looked like. She wasn't even sure how old he was. Why had she agreed to babysit when Mr. Winter approached her at the swim club? She had never seen him before, and it was flattering that he took her for being capable, as if just being a girl her age automatically qualified her as a babysitter.

By the time the Winters came home, Harriet had eaten most of the M&Ms in the glass bowl on their coffee table: first all the blue ones, then the red ones, then all the green ones, and so on, leaving, in the end, only the yellow.

They gave her too much money and didn't ask her about anything. Mrs. Winter seemed to be waiting for her to leave before checking on the baby. Mr. Winter drove her home in silence. When they reached her house he said, My wife. He hesitated, then he said, You understand, don't you? and Harriet answered, Yes, without looking at him or being sure what they were talking about, although she did really know what he was telling her, and then she got out of his car and watched him drive away.

1951

RICHARD BAUSCH

One catastrophe after another, her father said, meaning her. She knew she wasn't supposed to hear it. But she was alone in that big drafty church house, with just him and Iris, the maid. He was an Episcopal minister, a widower. Other women came in, one after another, all on approval, though no one ever said anything—Missy was seven, and he expected judgments from her about who he would settle on to be her mother. Terrifying. She lay in the dark at night, dreading the next visit, women looking her over, until she understood that they were nervous around her, and she saw what she could do. Something hardened inside her, and it was beautiful because it made the fear go away. Ladies with a smell of fake flowers about them came to the house. She threw fits, was horrid to them all.

One April evening, Iris was standing on the back stoop, smoking a cigarette. Missy looked at her through the screen door. "What you gawkin' at, girl?" Iris said. She laughed as if it wasn't much fun to laugh. She was dark as the spaces between the stars, and in the late light there was almost a blue cast to her brow and hair. "You know what kind of place you livin' in?"

"Yes."

Iris blew smoke. "You don't know *yet*." She smoked the cigarette and didn't talk for a time, staring at Missy. "Girl, if he settles on somebody, you gonna be sorry to see me go?"

Missy didn't answer. It was secret. People had a way of saying things to her that she thought she understood, but couldn't be sure of. She was quite precocious. Her mother had been dead since the day she was born. It was Missy's fault. She didn't remember that anyone had said this to her, but she knew it anyway, in her bones.

Iris smiled her white smile, but now Missy saw tears in her eyes. This fascinated her. It was the same feeling as knowing that her daddy was a minister, but walked back and forth sleepless in the sweltering nights. If your heart was peaceful, you didn't have trouble going to sleep. Iris had said something like that very thing to a friend of hers who stopped by on her way to the Baptist church. Missy hid behind doors, listening. She did this kind of thing a lot. She watched everything, everyone. She saw when her father pushed Iris up against the wall near the front door and put his face on hers. She saw how disturbed they got, pushing against each other. And later she heard Iris talking to her Baptist friend. "He ain't always thinkin' about the Savior." The Baptist friend gasped, then whispered low and fast, sounding upset.

Now Iris tossed the cigarette and shook her head, the tears still running. Missy curtsied without meaning it. "Child," said Iris, "what you gonna grow up to be and do? You gonna be just like all the rest of them?"

"No," Missy said. She was not really sure who the rest of them were.

"Well, you'll miss me until you *forget* me," said Iris, wiping her eyes.

Missy pushed open the screen door and said, "Hugs." It was just to say it.

When Iris went away and swallowed poison and got taken to the hospital, Missy's father didn't sleep for five nights.

Peeking from her bedroom door, with the chilly, guilty dark looming behind her, she saw him standing crooked under the hallway light, running his hands through his thick hair. His face was twisted; the shadows made him look like someone else. He was crying.

She did not cry. And she did not feel afraid. She felt very gigantic and strong. She had caused everything.

Little Brother™

BRUCE HOLLAND ROGERS

Peter had always wanted a Little Brother™. His favorite TV commercials were the ones that showed just how much fun he would have teaching Little Brother™ to do all the things that he could already do himself. But last Christmas, Mommy had said that Peter wasn't ready for a Little Brother™.

This Christmas morning when Peter ran into the living room, there sat Little Brother™ among all the wrapped presents, babbling baby talk, smiling his happy smile. Peter was so excited that he ran up and gave Little Brother™ a big hug around the neck. That was how he found out about the button. Peter's hand pushed against something cold on Little Brother™'s neck, and suddenly Little Brother™ wasn't babbling. Suddenly, Little Brother™ was limp on the floor, as lifeless as any ordinary doll.

"Careful!" Mommy said.

"I didn't mean to!"

Mommy picked up Little Brother™, sat him in her lap, and pressed the black button at the back of his neck. Little Brother™'s face came alive and wrinkled up as if he were about to cry. Mommy bounced him on her knee and told him what a good boy he was.

"Little Brother™ isn't like your other toys, Peter," Mommy said. "You have to be extra careful with him." She put Little Brother™ down on the floor, and he took tottering baby steps toward Peter. "Why don't you let him help open your other presents?"

So Peter showed Little Brother™ how to tear the paper and open the boxes. Peter's other toys were a fire engine, some talking books, a wagon, and lots and lots of wooden blocks. The fire engine had lights, a siren, and hoses that blew green gas just like the real thing. There weren't as many presents as last year, Mommy explained, because Little Brother™ was expensive. That was okay. Little Brother™ was the best present ever!

Everything that Little Brother™ did was funny and wonderful. Peter put all the torn wrapping paper in the wagon, and Little Brother™ took it out again and threw it on the floor. Peter started to read a talking book, and Little Brother™ came and turned the pages too fast for the book to keep up.

But then, while Mommy went to the kitchen to cook breakfast, Peter tried to show Little Brother™ how to build a tall tower out of blocks. Every time Peter had a few blocks stacked up, Little Brother™ swatted the tower and laughed. Peter laughed, too, for the first time, and the second. But then he said, "Now watch this time. I'm going to make it really big."

The tower was only a few blocks tall when Little Brother™ knocked it down.

"No!" Peter said. He grabbed hold of Little Brother™'s arm. "Don't!"

Little Brother™'s face wrinkled. He was getting ready to cry.

"Don't cry," Peter said. "Look, I'm building another one! Watch me build it!"

Little Brother™ watched. Then he knocked the tower down.

Peter had an idea.

When Mommy came into the living room again, Peter had built a tower that was taller than he was. "Look!" he said.

But Mommy just picked up Little Brother™, put him on her lap, and pressed the button to turn him back on. Little Brother™ started to scream.

"Peter!" Mommy scolded.

"I didn't mean to!"

"Peter, I told you! He's not like your other toys. When you turn him off, he can't move, but he can still see and hear. He can still feel. It scares him."

"He was knocking down my blocks."

"Babies do things like that," Mommy said. "That's what it's like to have a baby brother."

Little Brother™ howled.

"He's mine," Peter said too quietly for Mommy to hear. When Little Brother™ calmed down, Mommy put him back on the floor and told Peter to clean up the wrapping paper. She went back into the kitchen. Peter had already picked up the wrapping paper once, and she hadn't said thank you.

Peter wadded the paper into angry balls and threw them one at a time into the wagon until it was almost full. That's when Little Brother™ broke the fire engine. Peter turned just in time to see him lift the engine up over his head and let it drop.

"No!" Peter shouted. The windshield cracked and popped out as the fire engine hit the floor. Broken. Peter hadn't even played with it once, and it was broken.

Later, when Mommy came into the living room, she didn't thank Peter for picking up all the wrapping paper. Instead, she scooped up Little Brother™ and turned him on again. He trembled and screeched louder than ever.

"How long has he been off?" Mommy demanded.

"I don't like him! Take him back!"

"You are not to turn him off again. Ever!"

"He's mine!" Peter shouted. "He's mine and I can do what I want with him! He broke my fire engine!"

"He's a baby!"

"He's stupid! I hate him!"

"You are going to learn to be nice with him."

"I'll turn him off, if you don't take him back. I'll turn him off and hide him someplace where you can't find him!"

"Peter!" Mommy said, and she was angry. She was angrier than he'd ever seen her before. She put Little Brother™ down and took a step toward Peter. She would punish him. Peter didn't care. He was angry, too.

"I'll do it!" he yelled. "I'll turn him off and hide him someplace dark!"

"You'll do no such thing!" Mommy grabbed his arm and spun him around. The spanking would come next.

But it didn't. Instead he felt her fingers searching for something at the back of his neck.

Currents

HANNAH BOTTOMY VOSKUIL

Gary drank single malt in the night, out on the porch that leaned toward the ocean. His mother, distracted, had shut off the floodlights and he did not protest against the dark.

Before that, his mother, Josey, tucked in her two shivering twelve-year-old granddaughters.

"I want you both to go swimming first thing tomorrow. Can't have two seals like you afraid of the water."

Before that, one of the girls held the hand of a wordless Filipino boy. His was the first hand she'd ever held. They were watching the paramedics lift the boy's dead brother into an ambulance.

At this time, the other girl heaved over a toilet in the cabana.

Before that, the girl who would feel nauseated watched as the drowned boy's hand slid off the stretcher and bounced along the porch rail. Nobody placed the hand back on the stretcher, and it bounced and dragged and bounced.

Before that, Gary saw the brown hair sink and resurface as the body bobbed. At first he mistook it for seaweed.

Before that, thirty-five people struggled out of the water at the Coast Guard's command. A lifeguard shouted over Jet Ski motors about the increasing strength of the riptide.

Before that the thirty-five people, including Gary and the two girls, formed a human chain and trolled the waters for the body of a Filipino boy. The boy had gone under twenty minutes earlier and never come back up.

Before that, a lifeguard sprinted up the beach, shouting for volunteers. The two girls, resting lightly on their sandy bodyboards, stood up to help.

Before that, a Filipino boy pulled on the torpid lifeguard's ankle and gestured desperately at the waves. My brother, he said.

Before that, it was a simple summer day.

After

BILL KONIGSBERG

After, get in your car and drive. Turn up the heat. Blare music. Something with screeching guitars that drowns out any thought. Thinking is bad, after.

Watch the streetlights whiz by in your peripheral vision, and let their blurs trickle down the sides of your eyes. Think of them like tears. They are as close as you'll allow. You know that. You know.

Remember how you felt during, how you turned everything off, how you let your mind leave. You thought about, of all things, the white Tonka truck you used to love as a kid. You used to sleep with it. When the paint chipped, you had your mom take you to the hobby store to buy paint so you could touch it up. The white color you used wasn't quite right, but you loved that truck like it was your best friend.

Be careful not to go through a red light. Last time, you sped past a red on Broadwater. You were lucky no car was crossing the other way, or else you'd be dead. Yeah, real lucky. At home under your denim sheets that night, you'd wondered if maybe you'd forgotten about that light on purpose. In a flash, it could have been all over, and in the warmth of your bed you shuddered, thinking about what it would have felt like. After.

Slow down your driving. Stop on a yellow. Feel your forehead. Smooth. No blood. When they pushed your head into the side of the table, you thought maybe it would puncture, leave a scar. They were smarter than that. Both times, they only left marks under your clothes.

Mikey watched. So did Ethan. Your dad used to pick Mikey up and drive him to school with you, when you were in middle school, and you would sit in the back seat, texting dirty words to each other and seeing who cracked up first. Ethan used to come over after school and you'd wrestle. Mikey stopped talking to you when the rumor started. You're not sure, but Ethan may have started the rumor.

You simply don't know how anyone else could know about Joey. Ethan, he saw you guys. At Rimrock Mall. Joey is different, way. Ethan saw you together, and the next day at school was the first time. This was the second. You wonder if your pride can take a third without erupting in some dangerous way. You think possibly not.

Your elbow burns, bad. Last time they used lighters, burnt the hairs along your forearm. It scared you more than anything else. This time, a lit cigarette. Under your clothes. You don't want any marks that will last. You want to be a blank slate when you finally escape Billings, escape high school. Tabula rasa.

Pass the police station off Grand and 13th and ponder what would happen if you stopped there, pulled up your shirt sleeve, explained. Coach Donahue would freak. That's not what baseball players do. They don't squeal on teammates, they don't go all soft, and anyway, what good could come of it? If they arrested all those kids, you'd be the one who had them arrested. Everyone would hate you.

Besides, your family. You remember the time over dinner your dad made the joke about Coaches versus Cancer, a popular college basketball tournament.

"I'll take cancer," he said, and you cracked up because it was in such bad taste and your mom was sitting there staring at him, her mouth wide open. Then, somehow, the conversation turned political, and your dad's mustache twitched as he cut into his steak, and he said something you'd never forget.

"Tell you what, Ricky. You ever get the urge to come home and tell us you're gay, do me a favor. Have cancer instead. Tell me you have cancer."

You think of the burn on the tip of your elbow like a cancer splotch. What do they call them? Lesions. Maybe tonight you'll take your shirt off and show him your elbow and tell him it's cancer. He'll be so relieved. Family values.

Think about calling Joey. He's the one person who would get it. Think of his voice like caramel, glance in the rearview mirror, and catch yourself smiling, which surprises you. You expected a grimace, but the caramel voice in your imagination melted some of the anguish away. You will. You'll call him tonight. There are some things you can change, and some you guess you can't. Like in a million years. Caramel soothes burns. Burns don't ruin caramel.

Pull up to your house, turn off the headlights, and close your eyes for the moment before you pull the key from the ignition. Hold your breath. Count to ten.

The pain throbs in your elbow. You think about your mom and calamine lotion. When you were a kid. You wonder if you could just show her, no words, no explanations, and get her to sit on the side of the tub and rub calamine lotion on your elbow. That's what you want. You're sixteen, and you want your mom to stop what she's doing and soothe you, make it all better.

Step out of the car, head up the walkway, fumble for your key. Go for a blank expression when you open the door, and Mom is sitting there, on the couch, eating a bowl of Cheerios.

"Welcome home," she'll say, smiling, and the calamine dreams will fade away. Because you know. The price would be too high. After.

Accident

DAVE EGGERS

You all get out of your cars. You are alone in yours, and there are three teenagers in theirs, an older Camaro in new condition. The accident was your fault, and you walk over to tell them this.

Walking to their car, which you have ruined, it occurs to you that if the three teenagers are angry teenagers, this encounter could be very unpleasant. You pulled into an intersection, obstructing them, and their car hit yours. They have every right to be upset, or livid, or even violence-contemplating.

As you approach, you see that their driver's side door won't open. The driver pushes against it, and you are reminded of scenes where drivers are stuck in submerged cars. Soon they all exit through the passenger's side door and walk around the Camaro, inspecting the damage. None of them is hurt, but the car is wrecked. "Just bought this today," the driver says. He is eighteen, blond, average in all ways. "Today?" you ask.

You are a bad person, you think. You also think: what a dorky car for a teenager to buy in 2005. "Yeah, today," he says, then sighs. You tell him that you are sorry. That you are so, so sorry. That it was your fault and that you will cover all costs.

You exchange insurance information, and you find yourself, minute by minute, ever more thankful that none of these teenagers has punched you, or even made a remark about your being drunk, which you are not, or being stupid, which you are, often. You become more friendly with all of them, and you realize that you are much more connected to them, particularly to the driver, than possible in perhaps any other way.

You have done him and his friends harm, in a way, and you jeopardized their health, and now you are so close you feel like you share a heart. He knows your name and you know his, and you almost killed him and, because you got so close to doing so but didn't, you want to fall on him, weeping, because you are so lonely, so lonely always, and all contact is contact, and all contact makes us so grateful we want to cry and dance and cry and cry.

In a moment of clarity, you finally understand why boxers, who want so badly to hurt each other, can rest their heads on the shoulders of their opponents, can lean against one another like tired lovers, so thankful for a moment of peace.

Homeschool Insider:
The Fighting Pterodactyls

RON CARLSON

When we finally decided on homeschool for my sister, Joylene, and me, our first challenge was to select a mascot. After all, I'd been a Cougar at Big River Middle School and Joylene had been a Leopard at the high school, and now at our house who were we? We settled on the Fighting Pterodactyls, because it sounded terrific and used one of my spelling words. But there was something sad about knowing we didn't exactly have any rival schools. The Rubynars have homeschooling and so we did go over to their house and tell them they were our rival school, but it wasn't a good idea since they have seven kids and wanted to schedule a football season right away. Lloyd Rubynar chased us down the street with Joylene insulting him all the way, asking what was their mascot, what were their school colors, why don't they clean up their campus, things like that, things Lloyd would have a little trouble with.

I asked Joylene what our school colors were and she said, green and green, after our Plymouth and the color of our fridge, which is avocado, another spelling word.

Then, right off the bat during our first semester of homeschool, Joylene lost the hall pass. She'd already lost the living room pass, the garage pass, and the yard pass. Our teacher, Mrs. Yollstrom (our mother), put her in detention, and we both were unable to leave the kitchen table all day long. "I don't want you wandering the hallway without a pass," Mrs. Yollstrom told us. Mrs. Yollstrom's brother,

Uncle Todd, was on the couch as he had been for the two years that he's been under house arrest, sitting there with that monitor locked around his ankle, and Mrs. Yollstrom pointed at him as she had plenty of times before and said, "Do you want to end up like Uncle Todd? He didn't have a hall pass either!" She said we could earn it back by cleaning up the campus, which meant Joylene mowed the backyard and I swept the patio. It's a lovely campus in the fall with the sycamore leaves turning, the two old boats against the back fence, and the students (me and Joylene) strolling around with rakes and brooms.

So many things are the same here in homeschool as they were at Big River. There's no talking and you've got to keep your eyes on your own paper. From time to time I'll acciden-tally put a book report over a butter stain and grease it up pretty good, but Mrs. Yollstrom doesn't take points off for food marks. And if you're caught chewing gum, you have to spit it out or give some to the whole class, which is a good deal here since it's just one other piece.

The Pterodactyl Green on Green Junior Prom was a big disappointment for Joylene, but she shouldn't have got her hopes up. We had the radio in the den and big bowls of Doritos and we turned the lights down, but it wasn't too interesting. I'm in seventh grade and I don't dance. Mrs. Yollstrom was there as chaperone, standing in the corner. Uncle Todd wanted to dance, but Mrs. Yollstrom didn't allow it. There's a firm school policy about jailbirds. We finally just turned on *American Idol,* and Joylene cried quietly for a while, which was kind of like the prom anyway. She looked sweet in her green satin dress.

At the beginning of spring semester our brother, Dean, dropped out of Cornell and returned home to pursue his stud-ies at the other end of the kitchen table. He said homeschool was a natural for him. "There, the tuition was crushing, and I was looking for a smaller school anyway," he said. But he's worried that his degree in paleontology is going to take him longer here with us Pterodactyls because Dad has to spend so much time at the boat shop that Dean might not get all the quality tutorial and thesis and lab work he needs. It's fun to have him home, though—all our family together: Uncle Todd over on the couch in house arrest, Dean down the table in college, Joylene next to me in high school, and me in my chair studying fractions and Cuba with Mrs. Yollstrom, and learning the social skills necessary to survive in higher and higher education.

Forgotten

ANNE MAZER

They are going home. Two hungry, tired, dirty, and happy children are trudging home from the forest.

All day they followed paths, forded streams, and climbed trees. They discovered countries, crossed oceans and deserts, explored jungles teeming with life. They were animal and human, villain and hero, rich and poor, fearless and timid. They were born and died hundreds of times. New races of people spilled from their fingers. They tunneled under mountains, built and destroyed worlds, flew to the moon and sun, and reached the beginnings and ends of time.

They took so many forms, dreamed so many dreams, lived so many lives, that sometimes they forgot who they were supposed to be, or had been, or would become.

And when they were done, when they were content at last, when their faces were red from the sun, when their limbs were tired and their minds were empty, they set off for home. To eat warm, comforting food that their mother had made, be bathed and dressed in cool clean clothes that smelled of sun, and to lie down to sleep on soft white beds. To fall asleep under sheets that caressed their skin. They had dreamed all day and now their sleep would be a rest from dreams.

As they approach the house, the late autumn sun glows fiercely just above the mountains. The stars are not out yet.

The front windows cast a welcoming light as they run up the path toward the porch. They can already taste the good soup their mother has prepared, the hot milk and fresh bread.

They walk up the worn stairs to the door. One of them grabs the door handle and tries to turn it. It doesn't move. Mother must have locked it by mistake. That has happened before. They ring the doorbell and smile at each other as the sound echoes through the house.

No one answers.

They ring again. Perhaps she doesn't hear it.

"Mother! We're home! Your children are home!" The wooden door shakes as they bang on it.

Just as they begin to wonder if she has gone out, the baby cries. They hear their mother's footsteps on the stairs. In a moment, the baby stops crying.

Now they know their mother is near. Now is the time to call out and lean on the doorbell.

But still there is no answering call, no welcoming light in the hallway, no footsteps approaching.

They turn to each other with a frown. Isn't she looking for them, waiting for them, worrying about them?

They hear her voice now. She's singing to the baby. It's a tune that they've heard hundreds of times since their own infancies.

"Mother," they call out. "Mother!"

They call her again and again, until their throats ache and their voices fail, but still there is no answer. It is as though the air has swallowed their cries.

When a light comes on in the living room, they run to the window and pound on it, not caring if they break the glass or cut their fingers.

Their fists throb with pain, but the glass refuses to shatter.

In the living room, their mother carries their baby sister.

She stops to pick up a glass or a book or a pillow. When the baby fusses, she pats her gently.

"Mother!" they shout in hoarse, frantic voices. "Mother!"

She sets down the baby and walks to the window. For a moment, she looks right at them, right through them, as though they are not there, as though they do not exist.

"Mother!"

Their mother, who jumps at the baby's tiniest cry, doesn't blink or flinch. She yawns, then turns and walks across the room.

Stunned, the two children stare at each other.

Have they changed so that their mother no longer recognizes them? Is this what happened to their father? Is this why he never came back? Or, are they invisible now?

They pinch their fingers; they bite their hands. Slowly, they reach out to touch each other's faces.

They look and feel exactly as they always do, only dirtier and more tired . . . and they're scared.

As they shiver on the porch, their mother goes to the fireplace and lights a fire. They watch her hungrily, not daring to take their eyes away lest she too disappear.

When the fire is burning in the grate, she once again picks up the baby and bounces her up and down on her lap. Why does she see only the baby? The baby laughs and so does their mother as she plants kisses on the baby's round flushed cheeks and little delighted hands.

The sun sinks like a rock behind the hills. It's cold now and the children's thin coats don't keep out the wind. They look for an old blanket or rug, but the porch has been swept clean. Their neighbors are as distant as the stars. They are afraid to look at each other as hand in hand, they step off the porch.

The forest is closer now. They are there already. Earlier in the day it was a place of wonders. Now it's a place where the wind blows hard, where wild animals prowl, where sharp sticks and rocks wait to trip and cut them.

They have only the small comfort of each other's presence as they stand at the edge of the forest. But before they enter, they glance back one last time. Their house is no longer there. Is there anyone in this world who knows, who remembers them? They drop to their knees and crawl into the forest. They will search for leaves to burrow in under a ledge. Perhaps they'll find a withered apple or two on the ground or a few berries clinging to a thorny stalk. The forest stretches on forever.

After He Left

MATT HLINAK

It was an ordinary Monday morning except that she'd been up all night, crying. Trudging to school like a sleepwalker, she followed the familiar path without really meaning to, oblivious to the city coming to life around her. And then a sparrow plummeted from the cloudless summer sky onto the litter-strewn sidewalk in front of her. A sour breeze drifted out of the alley, ruffling the hand-sized bird's ash-colored feathers. People scurried around her while cars honked irritably at one another from the street. No one else saw the bird struggle back onto its feet before teetering over onto its back. No one else saw it kick its right leg for a moment, while its left leg lay still, as if riding half a bicycle. No one else saw it stop moving altogether. She slumped down beside the sparrow on the pavement and whistled softly, a faintly remembered lullaby from her childhood. And the world fluttered past them, as if they had never been there at all.

The Flowers

ALICE WALKER

It seemed to Myop as she skipped lightly from hen house to pigpen to smokehouse that the days had never been as beautiful as these. The air held a keenness that made her nose twitch. The harvesting of the corn and cotton, peanuts and squash, made each day a golden surprise that caused excited little tremors to run up her jaws.

Myop carried a short, knobby stick. She struck out at random at chickens she liked, and worked out the beat of a song on the fence around the pigpen. She felt light and good in the warm sun. She was ten, and nothing existed for her but her song, the stick clutched in her dark brown hand, and the tat-de-ta-ta-ta of accompaniment.

Turning her back on the rusty boards of her family's sharecropper cabin, Myop walked along the fence till it ran into the stream made by the spring. Around the spring, where the family got drinking water, silver ferns and wildflowers grew. Along the shallow banks pigs rooted. Myop watched the tiny white bubbles disrupt the thin black scale of soil and the water that silently rose and slid away down the stream.

She had explored the woods behind the house many times. Often, in late autumn, her mother took her to gather nuts among the fallen leaves. Today she made her own path, bouncing this way and that way, vaguely keeping an eye out for snakes. She found, in addition to various common but pretty ferns and leaves, an armful of strange blue flowers with velvety ridges and a sweetsuds bush full of the brown, fragrant buds.

By twelve o'clock, her arms laden with sprigs of her findings, she was a mile or more from home. She had often been as far before, but the strangeness of the land made it not as pleasant as her usual haunts. It seemed gloomy in the little cove in which she found herself. The air was damp, the silence close and deep.

Myop began to circle back to the house, back to the peacefulness of the morning. It was then that she stepped smack into his eyes. Her heel became lodged in the broken ridge between brow and nose, and she reached down quickly, unafraid, to free herself. It was only when she saw his naked grin that she gave a little yelp of surprise.

He had been a tall man. From feet to neck covered a long space. His head lay beside him. When she pushed back the leaves and layers of earth and debris Myop saw that he'd had large white teeth, all of them cracked or broken, long fingers, and very big bones. All his clothes had rotted away except some threads of blue denim from his blue overalls. The buckles of the overalls had turned green.

Myop gazed around the spot with interest. Very near where she'd stepped into the head was a wild pink rose. As she picked it to add to her bundle she noticed a raised mound, a ring, around the rose's root. It was the rotted remains of a noose, a bit of shredding plowline, now blending benignly into the soil. Around an overhanging limb of a great spreading oak clung another piece. Frayed, rotted, bleached, and frazzled—barely there—but spinning restlessly in the breeze. Myop laid down her flowers.

And the summer was over.

Homeward Bound

TOM HAZUKA

Thanksgiving, 1970, changing planes at a midwestern airport. I wasn't feeling thankful, not even for my sky-high draft lottery number. Eighteen years old, and I felt more guilty than good about luck shielding me from decisions I'd never wish on anybody: Canada, prison, Vietnam.

A soldier in a wheelchair was smoking Luckies like his life depended on it. He had a newspaper on his lap but wasn't reading it; I saw ashes on the headlines. After awhile two Marines sat down in front of me, discussing the football game. One hoped the storm would hold off because he hated goddamn turbulence.

A guy and a girl my age walked up to the wheelchair. "Vietnam?" the boy asked.

The soldier nodded.

"Good," she said. "Paralyzed, babyburner? Still got your manhood?"

"Yeah," he said, too quick, so quick it made you wonder.

The bigger Marine jumped up, but the skinny one shoved him aside. He dropped the kid with one punch, then smacked the girl twice in the face.

A security guard my father's age ran over. "Did you *see* that?" the girl shrieked.

"I saw it." The guard yanked the guy to his feet. "Now *get* outta here."

His voice was so venomous they fled without speaking.

The wheelchair soldier was shaking, pretending to read the paper. The Marines sat down again, careful, like they weren't sure the seats fit any more.

"Sorry, man," said the skinny one, his voice full of holes. "I was afraid you couldn't do it."

I remembered going to Niagara Falls as a kid, the disappointment of crossing into Canada and not feeling any different on foreign soil. It was like the world was just all one place.

We took off late in the snowstorm.

A Car

PIA Z. EHRHARDT

My father brought home a turquoise Porsche with red leather upholstery. My sister and I were small, eight and six, and fit tightly in the jump seats behind my parents.

We went for a ride, tooled around Rome, circled the Colosseum, showing off for the people looking. My father made us listen to him double-clutch because he said that this was good for the car. The sound of this felt like a struggle for the engine, a hesitation, and then the car sped on.

We'd parked along the Via Veneto, the car within eyeshot so my father and mother could admire it at the curb. My sister and I ordered gelati and my parents had coffees spiked with grappa. Everything alcoholic in Italy tasted like licorice.

We lived in an apartment building with a steep driveway, and the car stalled half a block from home. My father made us get out, and he pushed it, one hand on the steering wheel, the other on the open door. When he got to the top of the driveway he thought he would push it and then jump in, coast to the bottom, and park it in the underground garage, but when he pushed the Porsche, the car took off. He tried to hang on but it was heavy. The car dragged him and his shoes skidded along the driveway and my mother and sister and I watched in shock. I remember thinking then: You can't hold back a moving car.

The car went down the incline and over a wall and it fell two stories below onto a street that was usually filled with children. It fell obscenely with the bottom up, like a girl on her back with no underwear.

People came running from everywhere, and my father walked down, calmly, to look over the wall. No one was killed, but the car had flattened and my sister and I watched the tow truck pick it up, turn it over, and take it away. The pretty blue paint had scraped away, and the car was smashed up and gray.

My father never spoke about this and my mother didn't either, until they'd divorced and we were on her patio having a glass of wine. She'd admitted he'd been drinking, but that's all. Not that he had a trip-up on commonsense, shit logic—man, car, incline, fast, crash, death that escaped him that night—and for the next thirty years I was on the look-out for the other things he might do.

Stop

STEVE ALMOND

Or maybe you're here, in Sturbridge, Mass., off the pike, punching the register, Roy Rogers, a girl in a brown smock. America comes at you on buses, in caps and shorts, fuming. What the hell, you're killing each other, anyway. This kind of loneliness. What are words? You've got chores, duties, an inanimate world that needs you. Sometimes, late afternoon, you scrape the grill and figure: this could be love, this clean violence, the meaty shavings and steel beneath. There are other ideas out there, in magazines and movies, sweaters, perfume, bales of beautiful money. But you see your life, that which persists, the Dumpster out back, the counter dulled by your hands, relish troughs to fill. Some days the clouds are so thick they seem weighted. You are kind and not especially pretty. You do your job. You are polite. At great expense, you smile. Your best friend died just down the road, in an accident at night. You laid a pink bear before the marker and you persisted, you persist.

The Haircut

MANUELA SOARES

It was the haircut that sent Mom over the edge. When I walked in the door, she looked at me hard, the corners of her mouth turning down. Then she looked away, back at the potatoes in the sink. Last week she had absolutely forbidden me to cut it.

Upstairs in the bathroom, I studied my hair in the mirror—short. It made me feel a little exposed, but then running my hand through what was left made me smile.

No one in my family ever talks about anything important, so Mom stayed silently pissed and Dad acted like nothing had happened. I just wanted everyone to get over it. But then Mom started in.

"Your hair was so beautiful! Why you would hack it off like that is beyond me. You're such a beautiful girl—and now..."

My mother is aces at exasperation. You just don't want her to move over into mad. But that's what happened. My brother came home from college and laughed when he saw me—a nervous laugh that really upset Mom. Maybe it confirmed for her how bad the haircut looked—and reminded her that I'd disobeyed. My dad's in the army so we're all about discipline around here.

Mom blamed my friends Patty and Marilyn. She said there was something wrong with them because they have really short hair and don't use make-up. And oh yeah, they don't date. She thought they had too much influence over me—like I don't have a mind of my own. Maybe they did suggest I cut my hair, but I was tired of the way it looked; I wanted something different. I wanted my entire life to be different—maybe I just settled for a haircut.

Things were going to change soon and I wanted to be ready. In May I'd graduate high school. In the fall—college. Maybe Mom was worried about my leaving home. But I know how to take care of myself.

Mom started watching my every move and putting down Patty and Marilyn. It didn't help that I got home past curfew two weekends in a row after going to the movies with them. Suddenly, Mom said I couldn't go to a sleepover at Patty's that had been planned for weeks. How did she put it? "Until you learn how to tell time."

But the big problem was the prom. The three of us had decided to hold our own prom at Marilyn's. I knew I couldn't tell my parents. It was easier to pretend I was going to the school prom. That thrilled Mom no end.

On prom night, Dad dropped me off at school. Patty was waiting across the street in her silver VW. We went to Marilyn's and had a great party, dancing like crazy and eating this great food Marilyn's mother had left her for the week. Did I forget to mention that her parents were away? Actually, it was just me and Marilyn dancing. Patty hates to dance, but she likes being the DJ. Marilyn looked gorgeous in this deep red sheath of her mother's. Patty was wearing her usual uniform—jeans and a black T-shirt along with those big, round, wire-rimmed glasses that made her look like an owl. Later we had a pajama party, watching TV in Marilyn's parents' room on their king-sized bed and doing things that I hoped Mom would never find out about.

I got home at five in the morning and walked in on my parents yelling at each other in the kitchen. Somehow they'd found out I hadn't been at the prom. They stopped as soon as they saw me.

Dad said, "Sit down, young lady." He was mad. Mom was so upset she couldn't even speak. Dad doesn't like to yell and he didn't this time. He just told me how disappointed he was in me. That usually makes things worse, but for once it didn't change anything. I didn't regret a minute of that night.

In the end, I was grounded for the month until graduation and then sent to Grandma and Granddad's for the summer—away from all "bad influences."

Patty looked at me in disgust when I told her. "You're being sent to your grandparents? The ones with the big farmhouse, the woods, and the pond? How is that a punishment?"

Marilyn was grinning. "She'll be miserable 'cause she won't have us." She threw her arm around Patty and the two of them just stood there. They were losing me, but they still had each other.

* * *

That first week at my grandparents was really uncomfortable. They knew they were responsible for a "wholesome" atmosphere. But after I went fishing with Granddad a couple of times and then birding with Grandma, just like always, we all settled down.

The farm nearby rented out horses and Granddad took me to see the owner, Mr. Williams, about having one for the summer. We picked a sweet gray mare named Mavis.

"Do you want to ride her home?" Granddad asked. We were only a few miles away.

"I'd love to, Granddad, but I'm not sure how to get there."

"My daughter Sally can keep you company," Mr. Williams

volunteered. "She knows the trail real well. Go into the barn and she'll help you saddle up."

Sally was tall, with long copper-colored hair pulled back in a ponytail. She was wearing blue jeans, and her faded T-shirt said "Farm Boy." She turned her green eyes on me— and smiled.

I stammered a bit, but explained.

"Sure," she said. "Sounds like fun."

So we rode back to the house together, stopping every now and again as Sally pointed out a special place. We sat by a stream, the horses munching grass nearby, and talked. We liked each other. And I liked the way she looked at me. Suddenly I understood something about myself. Was this the change I wanted? Was this the different me?

It took all summer to find out.

What Happened During the Ice Storm

JIM HEYNEN

One winter there was a freezing rain. How beautiful! people said when things outside started to shine with ice. But the freezing rain kept coming. Tree branches glistened like glass. Then broke like glass. Ice thickened on the windows until everything outside blurred. Farmers moved their live-stock into the barns, and most animals were safe. But not the pheasants. Their eyes froze shut.

Some farmers went ice-skating down the gravel roads with clubs to harvest the pheasants that sat helplessly in the roadside ditches. The boys went out into the freezing rain to find pheasants, too. They saw dark spots along a fence. Pheasants, all right. Five or six of them. The boys slid their feet along slowly, trying not to break the ice that covered the snow. They slid up close to the pheasants. The pheasants pulled their heads down between their wings. They couldn't tell how easy it was to see them huddled there.

The boys stood still in the icy rain. Their breath came out in slow puffs of steam. The pheasants' breath came out in quick little white puffs. One lifted his head and turned it from side to side, but the pheasant was blindfolded with ice and didn't flush.

The boys had not brought clubs, or sacks, or anything but themselves. They stood over the pheasants, turning their own heads, looking at each other, each expecting the other to do something. To pounce on a pheasant, or to yell

Bang! Things around them were shining and dripping with icy rain. The barbed-wire fence. The fence posts. The broken stems of grass. Even the grass seeds. The grass seeds looked like little yolks inside gelatin whites. And the pheasants looked like unborn birds glazed in egg white. Ice was hardening on the boys' caps and coats. Soon they would be covered with ice, too.

Then one of the boys said, Shh. He was taking off his coat, the thin layer of ice splintering in flakes as he pulled his arms from the sleeves. But the inside of the coat was dry and warm. He covered two of the crouching pheasants with his coat, rounding the back of it over them like a shell. The other boys did the same. They covered all the helpless pheasants. The small gray hens and the larger brown cocks. Now the boys felt the rain soaking through their shirts and freezing. They ran across slippery fields, unsure of their footing, the ice clinging to their skin as they made their way toward the blurry lights of the house.

Coyote Bait

BRIAN BEDARD

From the bunk in her room just off the kitchen the little girl could see pieces of her parents moving, could hear talking in the kitchen on a sweltering August night. At first she couldn't tell what they were talking about, and then she saw the cat's tail twitching, curling around one of her father's knees.

"I haven't had any luck hunting the bastards, so I'm going to try Grandpa's method."

"I don't like the sound of it," her mother said.

"Nothing to it," her father said. "Just tie the cat to that post near the barn, then go sit in the dark, and wait."

"You mean you're going to leave him out there by himself so those coyotes can just come in and kill him?"

The little girl tensed in her bed, her eyes wide, watching the cat's spotted tail, her heart pounding with the realization of which cat this was.

"There won't be anybody killed but the coyotes," her father was saying. "Butch here will be on top of the post by the time the shooting starts."

"That's awful," her mother said. "It's cruel. And you'll scare Martha out of her wits."

"Nothing cruel about it. Grandpa did it for years. Never lost a cat. And the noise will glance off Martha like a thunderstorm passing in the night."

He swung around, and Martha could see one of the cat's eyes, a slice of its tail through the crack in the door.

"The thing to remember is that this is a barn cat, June. He knows how to take care of himself."

"You could sit up all night waiting."

"When Butch gets through making a fuss about being tied up, a whole family of coyotes will be sitting out there by the barn, trying to decide who goes first."

"I can't believe they'd be so dumb as to come right into the yard."

"I ain't arguing about them being smart. But they got a weakness. They like to eat cats."

"Don't I know it. That's probably what happened to Mickey and Max."

Martha frowned, pulled harder on the daisy appliqué she was peeling off her pajama top. They had told her the cats ran away. For a moment she was sickened by the thought of the coyotes dragging her cats into the wheat and eating them. Then she heard her mother closing cupboards and drawers, heard her father's boots on the linoleum as he moved toward the back porch. The kitchen light went off, and the house darkened. She climbed off the bunk, crossed the room, and parted the curtains to peer out at the back lot. She watched her father carry the cat out to the post in the silver white glare of the yard light.

Once the cat was secured, her father melded with the blackness. The cat remained, hunched on the ground, tail twitching in the dust. When the cat began to yowl, Martha pulled the curtains shut and hurried over to her bed.

She tried to close the yowling out, fixing her eyes on the tinfoil star she had made in school last Christmas. She thought of sleeping out on the porch where she could see the sky and the millions of blinking stars on quiet summer nights. She tried to remember the names of the constellations, but could only think of Big Dipper. She changed the picture in her head, saw the big calico the first time she had coaxed him out from under the porch of the hired man's house. He came slowly into the sunlight as he nosed toward the fish head she had tied to a long piece of rope.

She had lured him into the tool shed, then quickly closed the door. He didn't resist the doll clothes she had put on him, except for the bonnet, which he kept swiping at with his front paws. It was her favorite bonnet from her best doll, and she had hesitated using it, but it was the only one big enough to fit a cat's head. While she was taking the other clothes off him later that afternoon, he had bolted away with the bonnet still on his head and had torn it off somewhere in the fields. She'd been angry with him for a long time, but thinking about it now and hearing him yowling, she wasn't angry any more.

She turned over, closed her eyes, and tried to count sheep the way her grandmother Lewis had taught her. She counted as far as twenty-three when the air rocked with a rifle shot, then a second, and a third.

She was at the window in a flash, ears ringing as she scanned the brightly lit yard. She saw her father down on one knee, rolling two dead coyotes over, bloodspots spreading on their bellies and necks. The cat, scrunched into a ball at the top of the post, was watching silently as Martha's father dragged the coyotes over to his pickup and tossed them into the bed. Then he walked back to the post and lifted the cat down.

Martha's pulse was slowing; she thought he would let the cat loose now. Instead, he carried it into the house. The kitchen light came on, and she heard the refrigerator opening. Her father passed through the slit, carrying the cat and a bowl. The screen door slapped.

When her father came back in, turned the kitchen light out, and clomped up the stairs to his room, Martha got down from the bunk and opened her door, entering the dim kitchen. She crossed to the screen door and paused to peer out. At first, she couldn't see the cat, then she saw it crouched over the bowl of milk. In the heat-swollen quietness of the night, she could hear the rapid little licking sound around which the fields of wheat and the star-crowded sky seemed to hover.

Rapture

GAYLE BRANDEIS

The babysitter said the Rapture was coming and it was coming now. "Sorry you'll be left behind, Jew boy," the baby-sitter said, even though his charge—namely me—was a girl. He unfolded himself from the couch where we had been watching *Let's Make a Deal*. A man in a lobster suit had just won a donkey, a real donkey hitched to a cart and wearing a sombrero. I wondered if the lobster-man actually had to bring the donkey home. I wondered if the game show people taught him how to take care of it.

"Gotta go!" the babysitter said. "Gotta go to God!" He saluted me, clicked the heels of his white tennis shoes, and ran out the door.

I watched him race past the bay window, his arms waving over his head, his face upturned, laughing, like he was run-ning to catch a bus, a bus that was going to take him to the best summer camp ever.

I called my mom at the insurance office where she worked. "What's the Rapture?" I asked. The only place I knew the word from was a Blondie song that was on the radio a lot in those days. The way Blondie sang the word scared me—kind of slow and drawn out, like she was falling asleep. And then there was a weird part I didn't really understand about an alien eating cars. I hoped an alien wasn't going to come eat our Cutlass Ciera now that the Rapture was here.

"Is Daniel reading the Bible to you again?" she asked.

"No," I said, even though he had read a freaky passage to me earlier that day about a lady riding a serpent.

"It's a Christian thing," she said. "At the end of the world, Jesus is going to come take all the Christians away or something like that."

"What happens to the rest of us?" I asked.

"We all die a fiery death, I guess. I have to go, Janie. Be good." She hung up. She hung up on me even though we were both about to die. The phone squawked and squawked, like when the Emergency Broadcast System blats on the radio for a tornado or a flood. When I set the phone in its cradle, the quiet was almost more alarming. I looked out the window. The street was completely empty. The leaves on the trees were completely still. All the Christians were probably gone already. The fireball was probably on its way.

On *Let's Make a Deal*, a woman in an angel costume chose what was behind door number three. It was a boat, a glittery blue powerboat. She climbed up into the boat and I could see the jeans under her white angel robes. I could see her white tennis shoes, too, just like Daniel's. Christian tennis shoes. She waved to the camera and I knew she was waving at me, waving goodbye.

Alone

BRYAN SHAWN WANG

While Jun Chen lay before me, motionless and silent, and Bobbie screamed, "We only meant to scare him, jackass!" and Andrew murmured, "Oh Christ Oh Christ Oh Jesus Christ," I reflected on how the situation would have differed had I been alone, unchained from the others, free to act without regard to the expectations, or what I believed to be the expectations of Bobbie and Andrew and everyone else in this white-bread town—that, for instance, when the Hackett brothers, drunk and angry, skidded up my driveway in their beat-up Corolla, I would walk outside and greet them with a high five and a dopey smile; when Andrew scowled and called me yellow, after they detailed their evening plans and I hesitated for a moment, I would throw open the door and scrunch into the back seat, saying, "Ride on, cowboys"; when Bobbie turned around, his jowly face all grins, and asked, "Where to, Kemo Sabe?" I would suggest cruising Taylor Street to have some fun with Jun; when we passed him near his place on North Taylor and neither Bobbie nor Andrew recognized him, I would say, "There's our outlaw"; and when they badgered poor Jun into the car, I would flick him a cheesy thumbs-up and wink to put him at ease—for indeed, throughout this regrettable incident, I did not act according to my own designs but rather to satisfy such presumptions, to demonstrate to Andrew and Bobbie that I was anything but yellow, that outward appearances can deceive, that I deserved their company—this desire was what compelled me to join them, instructed me to lead them to Jun, shoved Jun from the car we parked behind the Old Towne strip mall, discovered the section of metal pipe and placed it in my hand, and when the pipe's bulk proved unwieldy, wrapped my other hand around, as well, and finally raised the club and brought it down not once, not twice, but twenty-one times on the only other chink in town: a man who had also spent his life stared at and mocked and pitied and ostracized and, in the end, merely reminded, day after day, of that irreparable and undeniable flaw, not unlike the hunched back, the deformed and unfinished body, the grotesque face and the mask that covers but does not conceal, a flaw that forever deprived him of anonymity, of associations untainted by prejudice, of self-assuredness and self-acceptance—and despite this, despite their culpability in all that had transpired, what Bobbie and Andrew Hackett believed as they fled was that I, Derek Wai, the lanky oriental kid they once had bullied but then respected, even liked, had simply gone berserk, and then they tore off into the night to leave me and Jun alone.

Head Case

NANCE VAN WINCKEL

In fairy tales, the one who looks back at you from the mirror is the one who possesses the heavy-duty, otherworldly secrets. That's how I felt about the one staring at me from the mirror in the women's latrine. Her eyes flashed a potent mix of pity and loathing. She had cornrows—with beads!—in her blond hair. A blue-eyed girl. Gazing at myself, I knew I looked ridiculous.

Bright moonlight streams in though the open tent flap. Soon I will get up and go with the older Tent 5 girls, who are from Scotland and speak a language I mostly understand, to feed spoonfuls of a mush we call cuss-turd into the mouths of several sad, ailing, elderly survivors. These people have lovely black eyes and caramel hands. One has a dislocated shoulder, another a broken wrist.

The Scottish girls call me Peaches. It's the color of the nail polish I'm wearing. I have no idea how it came to be on my toenails. We look down at our feet and go silent as we pass tents 9 and 10, inside which are the dead and almost-dead.

"Peaches, your green-shirt lady still can't get with that custard," the girl named Jenna says as soon as we're inside the oldsters' tent. The woman has not taken off her green shirt—and won't . . . no matter what quasi-cleaner-one is offered to her. Now she's shaking her head *No* to the Swiss Red Cross man who's holding the plastic container before her.

I slip it from his hand and kneel down. Did he think she'd

be able to open it on her own? I watch his legs move to the next person. He's new. He's still expecting hope, gratitude.

The woman points to her closed mouth and winces.

"Still," I say, "you need to eat." I fill a spoon with the gruel. She makes a face anyone would recognize as "yuck," but she lets me put the spoon into her mouth. High-calorie sustenance. The food, in a blue basket, dropped down to us from a helicopter. When the chopper turned and rattled back across the eerily quiet Andaman Sea, we saw the big red cross on its side. It headed south, toward Banda Aceh, where we'd heard the devastation was worse.

I don't recall grabbing onto palm branches. But this is what they've told me. Hotel Bulbul is no more. Kaput. *Kaput* is what the kids say about the boats washed ashore and the cars atop the pile of sticks that had been their school. Standing near these sticks and smashed desks, the kids stare at a tattered soggy map of the world. The North Pole is kaput. The inks of many countries have bled into one another.

Lying on grass mats with blue sheets pulled up to their chins, the Scottish girls whisper in the dark. They think I'm sleeping when I'm not. Dead to the world, they say. What a head case.

This morning, on the Scottish girls' radio, we heard men explain shifting tectonic plates. The voices sounded smoothed over by facts: the quake's rating and from exactly how far below the sea it must have come to heave the water so high.

Although the young Red Cross doctor claims to be Danish, he calls me Fraulein Peach. He asks, "Do you want to go home?"

"I don't know," I say.

"Think about it," he tells me. "The answer will come to you."

What comes to me is that I might have—as the girl I used

to be—mustered up a little crush on him. She would do that, I think. She was just that type.

The nurse comes by and says she'll unbraid my hair and we can give it a good washing, better than the "cursory" one my head had while I was "blotto." I touch the shaved place where my ten little stitches feel like plastic netting.

"Maybe tomorrow," I say, which is what I said yesterday.

I learn about flocculation. Add the aluminum sulfate, stir for five minutes, dump the water through the sand filter, and mix in the chlorine. The sweet doctor's hands show me how. Voilà. I can't say for sure, but I don't think whoever I'd been before would do this.

The truth is every day I feel less sure, not more, about who I am. My age, for instance. Maybe I'm not eighteen, which is what I feel. Jenna says if I were a dog, we could hazard a better guess. Her father's a veterinarian and he's shown her how to check the wear on a dog's molars.

What I *do* remember. I am told to concentrate on this.

This: how no one could walk away from the sea, how it came for everyone. The frothy white loveliness before anyone realized what the wave was, what it intended to do.

Men in yellow hardhats spraying disinfectant on the white plastic-wrapped bodies.

Fires against the night skies, that backdrop of constellations—stars that feel cruel to me now, spiteful.

The unnumbered tent. Its stacks of unfilled coffins. Waiting, waiting.

The soap will hurt, I know, when it hits the stitched-up hole through which a part of me has leached out.

Jenna and Karen come out of Tent 12, crying. No one in there was supposed to die, so as soon as I see the girls' faces I am crying too. Those are *our* charges. The girls take my hands.

"It's Green-lady." Jenna wipes her face with her shirttail. "Dr. Z says we should wait here."

"Wait with us." Karen squeezes my hand.

We wait. A boy named Sun squats by my knee. I'm wishing I'd stayed longer with the old woman, wishing I'd unloaded more spoonfuls of the awful gruel into her ravaged mouth. I feel a small cool finger cross my big toe's nail, and when I glance down, I see that Sun is scratching off the few specks of color—like a light dusting of coral— that remain.

Friday Night

ELIZABETH EHRLICH

Yesterday I asked Mom, "Could I sleep at Anna's in the city tomorrow night?"

I knew Mom didn't want me to go out on Friday night. Friday night is Shabbat. Mom lights candles and my family eats dinner at home. We're not allowed to watch TV, just read or maybe play Scrabble. It's boring.

In high school everyone goes out on Friday night.

Anna just started at the same school as me. I live in the suburbs and Anna lives in New York City. We go to a private school halfway between. They live in an apartment and they're not Jewish. Otherwise, we're very similar.

I assured Mom I would go straight home with Anna after school and call the second we got there. I promised I would keep my cell phone in my pocket. I agreed to pay attention on the subway.

I mean I am already fourteen. I'm in high school. Anna has been taking the subway alone for years.

"Please, Mom," I argued. "I have been having Shabbat dinner my entire life, but I've never slept over in New York City."

Everyone is more scared of the city now. Two weeks ago, on September 11, 2001, terrorists crashed two airplanes into the World Trade Center. The Twin Towers collapsed. People were jumping out of windows and pushing to get down a hundred flights of stairs. A lot of people died inside the Towers and firemen died trying to rescue them.

It was the second day of school when it happened. When I got home, Mom had it on TV and they kept showing the Towers coming down over and over.

Dad used to work near the Twin Towers, but he lost his job in August—before school started and right after Grandpoppy died—so Dad wasn't in the city that day. At my new school, one girl's mom died in the attack and another kid's dad is still missing.

"Will Anna's parents be home?" Mom asked me, about the sleepover.

Later, when I went by the kitchen, she was talking to Dad. First she said, "How are we going to pay the tuition?" Then she blew her nose and said, "I didn't think she would grow up so fast."

"We should let her go," Dad replied.

Mom has been crying every day since Grandpoppy died. It's been over a month. After the funeral, Mom sat *shivah* for her dad. She stayed in the house for a week. People visited and brought food. We covered the mirrors so we wouldn't be vain. It was a million degrees in the house because we don't have air conditioning.

On the last day of *shivah,* Dad lost his job. The next day, Mom and I went shopping for school supplies. The bill was almost three hundred dollars and Mom burst into tears in front of everyone at the checkout. Dad doesn't do embarrassing stuff like that.

Mom goes to synagogue every day now to say *kaddish* for Grandpoppy. *Kaddish* is a prayer that says how great and exalted God is. You're supposed to recite it when someone dies, even though that's probably when you don't believe in

God the most. It's pretty hard to exalt God when your dad dies or terrorists kill thousands of innocent people.

You think: either God doesn't care or He can't do anything about it.

For example, Grandpoppy's whole family was killed in the camps and he alone survived. In the hospital, before he died, I asked him, "Did you still believe in God after that?"

"I didn't have nothing," he mumbled. "God was all I had."

But on September 11, and the whole week after, the sky was so blue and clear; it was like you were trying to look into God's eyes and they were just blank.

Mom finally said I could sleep over at Anna's.

After school we take the subway. It goes along a high track, then dives underground. We climb up the stairs to the street and it's suddenly so bright.

Anna has a doorman and an elevator. Her apartment has huge pictures on the wall and they have a dog. We don't have a dog even though we have a backyard.

After a while, Anna and I go out to dinner on our own. By then it's dark. There are fifty restaurants right on her block. The minute we sit down my cell phone rings. I apologize to Dad because I forgot to call home.

Dad says, "Well, Shabbat Shalom."

I say, "You too." It would feel funny to say it back, with Anna here in the restaurant.

On the way out, I take matches for a souvenir. Outside, the air is warm and soft. There are so many people on the street, it's like all the buildings have turned inside out.

We walk in a river of people. We walk a long time to the memorials. There are huge boards with posters and notes tacked up. There are pictures of weddings and people in uniforms. "Hero," they say, or "Missing." We walk around the park. There are musicians and people reading poems out loud and you can smell incense. I hug Anna for all the people who died. This is the most important night of my life so far.

I didn't know you could sit down right on a sidewalk. We sit in front of a sign propped up on the ground. "José—In Heaven," it says, over a picture of a man holding a baby. It's like a shrine with a bunch of plastic flowers, candles all around and some beads with a cross.

"It's a rosary," Anna whispers.

"I know that," I whisper back.

One candle is blown out. I look for my matches. My cell phone is not in my pocket. It's not in any of my pockets.

It takes three matches before one catches fire. I light my candle and watch it burn.

Please find all the missing people and my phone.

Beyond Yesler

PETER BACHO

One day, Cortez—first name or last, no one knew—suddenly declared himself to be the baddest young brother in the Yesler Terrace housing project. To prove it, he snuck up on Bobby Vincente, called out his name and sucker-punched him when he turned around.

"High-yella punk," Cortez snorted as he and his pals fished through Bobby's pockets for change. "If I was you, I'd stay where you are."

It took two weeks, but Paulie, Bobby's older brother, caught up with Cortez and broke his knee with a baseball bat. Bobby was glad, but unlike Paulie, he didn't love fighting—the pain, the jumbled emotions. It just wasn't him.

The differences didn't end there. Bobby was also much lighter than Paulie, which was hard to figure since his Filipino father was the color of old mahogany and his mother was part black.

But differences aside, the boys were close—Paulie ever vigilant, Bobby ever grateful. Bobby knew he'd avoided many more battles because the thugs knew they'd have ferocious Paulie to deal with later.

That was over now because Paulie had become an accidental soldier, an eighteen-year-old draftee. Last month, a Viet Cong mortar turned him into a statistic.

When word got out, a lot of neighbors came around—

some to offer condolences, but others, Bobby was certain, to make sure Paulie was dead.

In the days following the funeral, Bobby's neighbors would nod solemnly, their demeanor acknowledging his loss. But eventually that changed, especially for the girls, because life goes on, and, well, Bobby was handsome, even pretty—a mixed blessing on the street.

It's what Angie Tavares thought. She was an older and very pretty Filipino-Indian girl, who lived in the apartment two doors down. As far as Bobby could tell, she spent her time teasing her thick, black hair so that a few strands always defied gravity, standing up and curling at the ends.

Earlier today Angie had stepped out from her doorway and stopped him on his way to the downtown library, his Saturday destination. He loved the feel of the books, the silence of the reading room. Saturday was his chance to imagine, to explore the world beyond Yesler.

At first Bobby hadn't noticed Angie, so intent was he on balancing four thick novels. He almost walked into her, but pulled up just in time.

"Oh, hi," Bobby said.

Angie smiled, then put her index finger daintily on his jacket lapel. "Bobby," she began coyly. "You look like Smokey . . . as in Smokey Robinson."

And ooh, baby, baby, her folks were out so could he please come over and croon falsetto lyrics of love?

He looked at her, his eyes bouncing inside his head. She was pretty enough. No, make that real pretty, but . . .

"I gotta return these books, otherwise there's fines and well, you know," he finally blurted, as he turned to walk away.

"If you ever wanna come over to talk . . . " he heard her say. "I'm sorry 'bout Paulie."

"Me, too," he mumbled.

Bobby declined the invitation. He may have been the only boy in Yesler to have ever turned Angie down. Today, though, he just wasn't interested, or at least not interested enough.

He'd heard the whispers—that he was *that way*—but he ignored them. He didn't dislike Angie or any other girl, but he wasn't fond of what it took to get and keep them—the loud talking, fist-throwing, territory-establishing rituals that other boys did.

Just last week he'd watched two boys punch and gouge each other in a nearby park until hoots from the spectators caught a passing cop's attention. From Bobby's perch on the edge of a knoll, he saw Luisa—the object of their combat—slowly drift to the back of the crowd and leave with Eddie, the street-savvy half-brother of a Mexican friend of his.

Luisa smiled as she passed him. "Shh," she said.

Silly, he thought, too much mess—way too much, especially for the young women, whose main value seemed to be their skill at making their unfaithful lovers feel good about themselves. He'd seen it happen too often. They would be left holding diapered surprises and having even less chance of changing their lives and leaving Yesler.

It happened to Angie, who gave birth to twins a year or so ago. No sign of the kids since. Word had it they'd been sucked up by the state.

And now she was ready to risk it all again. Bobby thought she was foolish, but not that different from a lot of the other Yesler girls he knew.

"Get over here," Bobby had often heard streetwise Romeos snarl at Angie and other young women. But it wasn't just the words that stung his ears, it was the universal tone, like a master summoning his dog. If that was all he wanted, he'd have gone to the pound and adopted a beagle or some Lassie lookalike.

Bobby expected more, or maybe it was less—he wasn't sure. He figured that having a girlfriend should be simpler and fairer—two people meeting, finding out they liked each other, deciding to be together, deciding to be apart.

That's why entertaining Angie was the farthest thing from his mind. He knew how she and the other Yesler girls would expect him to be, and that wasn't him.

Bobby quickened his pace. In his mind he could see the reading room, he could hear the silence: his oasis—no Cortez, no confusion, no sorrow or doubt. With Paulie gone, he'd have to figure out who he was—and who he wasn't—on his own. He knew Angie couldn't help him, but maybe—just maybe—the library could.

Half Sleep

MATT KRAMPITZ

Yates was the kind of kid who picked spiders off the floor and threw them outside. He was gentle always and he spoke to me like I was an adult. He played piano and sang like Elton John and he told stories that made everyone laugh even though they always ended badly. Most importantly, he was my brother.

When my parents would go out he and his friends would watch me. They played basketball and drank beers in the driveway. I kept score and shot steady free throws for both sides. He didn't smile often, but when he did it was real.

When I started sixth grade he finished high school. We had a big barbecue planned, but he only stayed for a minute and then drove off with his friends to do what my parents called "God knows what." He was never home before midnight and he moved out that winter. Our house calmed down after that. For months it had been building with the weight of unasked questions. My parents wanted him to at least stay truthful. I only knew that he barely spoke anymore and got irritated if he spent more than two hours with me.

Things started disappearing. My father said it was possible he had left his cordless drill on a job site. Then his miter saw was gone as well. My mother lost some money or at least couldn't remember spending it. My father sat on the couch with his head tilted toward the ceiling thinking of places the money could have gone. He wondered out loud if my mother had gotten her nails done or made a trip to the grocery store or been mugged. She fumed back that it doesn't cost ninety dollars to get her nails done. I remember sitting in the living room listening to hushed voices snapping from the kitchen. Yates stopped coming to the house.

One late night, before they changed the locks, I heard the squeak of a hinge and the brush of weather stripping sweep the wood floor. I knew it was my brother by the creep of his steps. He padded lightly, heel first, toward the kitchen. I heard drawers roll open and the woolly jingle of junk being moved. The drawers closed and the footsteps continued, eluding the creaky seams. My heart was a gong in my half sleep.

The hollow door of my room swung slowly and I noticed a change in light and breeze. I could feel his presence in the doorway. Though it was too dark to see, I could envision his greasy brown hair that turned blond some summers and his big sad eyes. I could almost smell him, his smell, like the must of a cabin and stale menthol cigarettes.

His steps led to my window and to the acoustic Gibson Hummingbird that leaned by the sill. It was my father's guitar. The one he had taught Yates on and that Yates had promised to teach me on. I could picture his thick fingers with the nails bit down to nubs working the neck of the guitar. Those same fingers were now reaching to take it away.

I didn't stop him. I imagine I could have, but I didn't, and I kept the guitar's disappearance from my parents for months because I didn't want them to be wounded like I was and like Yates was. All I told them was that I knew he still loved us and that he was hurt as we were hurt. What I

never told them—to spare them the agony of strict detail—
was that when he left the room I could feel his presence in
the doorway for a long while, staring at me as I slept, as if he
wanted me to wake up, and then I heard the gush of a broken throat and the soft chirping breath of his tears.

No Wake Zone

L. C. FIORE

On the last day of summer, Adham and his mother and his father took the ferry from the city to the Toronto Island Park, where they often went to picnic and to pedal paddle boats along the shore. Near the boxwood maze they heard the whimpering of an animal and beneath a rose bush discovered a dog with only three legs. Its fourth leg was a nub that seemed never to have grown. They waited with the dog for a short time before deciding it belonged to no one, that someone had left it there to chance. His father had never allowed pets, but the dog followed them, hobbling, past the carousel and the pony rides, down to the docks. There, his father slipped a chain from a piling and led the dog across the gangplank, where, on the viewing deck of the ferry, it sat patiently while the family watched the harbor slide into the mist.

Adham's mother positioned him at the corner of the railing where the wind wrapped his slacks around his legs. She licked her fingers and smoothed his cowlick before turning her camera over in her hands. She was finishing a roll of film.

Be a good boy and smile for me, she said. Smile for *umayma*.

She bent down, trying to capture both him and the skyline in the frame. The hem of her dress lifted, just slightly, and Adham hoped no one was watching. He did not want anyone to see his mother that way, her hair blowing, her lips slightly parted, and her stockings slick across her knees.

I need this picture to remember you by, she said. So soon you will be going off to school.

But his father seemed not to notice. He was standing at the rail, smoking a cigarette. He cupped the cigarette in his hand, and Adham watched him raise his fingers to his lips and draw smoke from his palm as if fanning the embers there, as if were he to open his hand the fingertips would be lit with countless, miniature pyres. Adham imagined himself lifted within the inhale and the exhale; he wanted to be drawn in below his father's mustache, welcomed into his father's lungs to hear the heartbeat, the stomach acids, and the death rattle of the bronchi. He wanted to sleep there nestled against his father's spirit before the exhale dissipated the boy across the water.

I've got you on film now, his mother said. I've captured you inside this camera.

Above their heads, near the smokestacks, the national flag wavered against the washed-out sun. The pilot blasted the ferry horn. Adham turned to the rail, not crying—he was too old for that—though the patrol boats on the water and the bridge into the city were diffracted as if a painter had rubbed the still-wet canvas with his thumb. His image was on the film and he felt a dread of moving on, inevitability like a swelling wave: at school there would be newness and pining. The night before, they'd gone to dinner at the home of a family friend. He and the daughter, Nadia, were sequestered in the kitchen, as if they were five years old again, unmannered. She attended boarding school in Québec and was one year ahead. Her family was strict Muslim and made her cover her hair when she was home. He groped for conversation while she described biology class and what he might look forward to, the way she had plunged her scalpel into the eye of a fish to find the waxy ball beneath the pupil. She described the smell of the formaldehyde and when the word was formed it wafted over their lamb *patcha* and *kadee* loaf and turned the offering sour, like the preservation of things long dead.

One more photograph, his mother said. Once more and then we'll go inside.

His father spun his cigarette into the jetsam and the waves. He came to stand beside his boy along the rail. Adham ran his fingers through the dog's coarse hair and the dog looked up at him, mournful. His mother took one final picture of the father and son, the dog at their side. Adham would keep this photograph pinned inside his letter jacket to remind him of choices, the weight of decisions, and of home.

What should its name be? his father asked.

Jonam, Adham said, because it meant *my life* and it was what his mother sometimes called him when she tucked him into bed.

You can visit on holidays, she promised.

His father placed his hand on his son's shoulder, and Adham stiffened beneath the touch. He wiped his face with his sleeve and the wetness bled into the cloth. He tried to breathe the mucus back inside his head.

His father said, I shared a room with Nadia's father, when we were new to this country. Until we found money enough to live on our own. Until I could send for your mother and your mother could bring you to me.

Do you remember? his mother asked.

Adham did not remember, not very well. He'd been too young. All that he knew of Iran was what his mother told him, about the boat they owned there, not a ferry or a ship but a little sailboat they'd take out spring and summer.

We never spoke of our families, his father said. But it was all we thought about. Our thoughts gave us strength.

The ferry came along the landing where the people waiting there were silhouettes against the dying light, steam rising from their coffee cups. Those on the dock waved; already, inside the cabin, passengers moved to the stairs. The dog barked once and bristled as it stood. It shook its head, and rattled its collar-chain, a rattle of keys, a door unlocked, water he would never cross again.

The Teacher's Son

AARON HAMBURGER

In the half-year that Mark Taborsky had been a student at Hebrew Academy, he'd made more friends than I ever had at the school I'd gone to my entire life. Partly this was because his mother, Mrs. Taborsky, was our new English teacher. Also, he knew all the right movies to see, sports to watch, Wii games to play, and the right things to say about them. He could hit and throw and catch balls. He was the first kid in our grade with an iPhone. He had golden brown hair and blue eyes. Also, he was a spectacularly unkind person. (How else did you get to be popular?) He took particular relish in mocking students with crude insults that seemed startlingly original, though they were generally the same thing: girls were sluts, and boys were girls.

Somehow I believed Mark's cruelty was born of some unexpressed psychic pain that I could coax him to reveal if I could get the two of us alone. My first chance to test my theory came when Mrs. Taborsky chose us two to travel to the gym storage room to return some orange traffic cones she'd used to illustrate run-on sentences. I found the whole exercise juvenile, but everyone else enjoyed it, especially Mark, who, while posing as a semicolon, tripped three different boys with his laceless Converse sneaker and muttered the magic words, "Flying faggot!" One boy indeed went flying and, while Mark watched with a satisfied smirk, almost sliced his forehead on the edge of a desk.

Careful with the horseplay," Mrs. Taborsky called out nervously from the board, her chalk squeaking out a dependent clause.

Clutching my orange cones to my chest, I pondered the miracle of walking down the hall by Mark's side. My mind went blank until we disappeared into the dusty-smelling storage room, and I mustered the courage to ask, "How did you like *The Scarlet Letter?*"

Mark, busy shoving a sack of red rubber dodge balls and field hockey sticks under a shelf of out-of-date prayer books, snarled, "What?"

Just then I hated him. He didn't deserve everything he had. Like a mother who encouraged him to read. And a God who'd given him beautiful blue eyes.

"Oh, you mean that book thing?" Mark went on. "Boring."

He was pure evil. Pure...boy. Anything that didn't involve the possibility of physical injury was boring. And we who were more sophisticated in our tastes were girls. "Boring, how?" I asked.

"Just boring," he replied with his usual eloquence.

"Yeah, you're right." I tried not to choke on my own words. "Why did your mother..." It felt thrillingly naked to refer to Mrs. Taborsky as his mother, "give us that stupid book to read?"

"Shut up about my mother, you faggot," he said.

There it was, my punishment for committing the sin of conversation. So I kept my mouth shut until all the orange cones were put away. But for some reason, we weren't leaving the storage room. "Have you ever done anything with girls?" asked Mark, blocking the door.

I told him I had.

"With who?"

"*Whom,* not *who,*" I said on instinct, then came up with a name: "Adrienne Cohen." Adrienne had been my babysitter when I'd required the services of a babysitter.

"Never heard of her."

I thought fast. "She's my neighbor. Once I asked her to meet me at Abercrombie to go shopping."

Mark burst out laughing. "You're lying," he said.

"Honestly," I said.

"No one meets anyone at Abercrombie," he said, the flicker of a smile playing at the corners of his lips. "Tell me the truth. I'll have so much more respect for you if you say, 'Mark, okay, I was lying. I never asked anyone to meet me at Abercrombie. I don't even know anyone named Adrienne Cohen.'"

"I really do know her." Unfortunately, my voice cracked.

"So what did you do with this Adrienne?" he said in a vaguely threatening tone.

I shrugged.

"You didn't do anything."

"Aren't we done here?" I said. "Can't we go?"

I reached past him for the door, but he blocked my way. "Not yet, fag," he said.

How had he guessed about me? I'd worked so hard all these years to disqualify myself, to hide behind the sidelines.

"Do what I tell you," he said. "Or I'll tell everyone about who you are."

For the first time in my life, my grades in English plummeted below the failing mark, but I didn't care. I got very quiet, even surly, just like Mark (who continued meeting me in the storage room, the only place he acknowledged my existence). The kids in school who never noticed me noticed it. Even my parents noticed it. And then, one day, while I was hiding in the library during recess, I ran into Mrs. Taborsky, who said she'd noticed it, too.

"I sense you've got so much bottled up inside," she sighed. "We're waiting for you to let it out."

And then it occurred to me that in some way, Mrs. Taborsky was my mother-in-law. In fact, someday she might become like my real mother-in-law. Mark and I would outgrow our storage room, and maybe in college we'd move in together, share an apartment. And I'd cook for him, even though I didn't know how.

"You must be a good mom," I blurted out.

She seemed puzzled. "Really? I mean, thank you. What makes you say that?"

"Because your son . . . I like your son." I couldn't say any more.

She touched my shoulder. "Be kind to him," she said. "He acts tough, but he's just a little boy."

"What do you mean?" I asked.

"I know," she whispered, then moved past me and into the hall, toward the forbidden territory of the teachers' lounge. And as I stared at her back, I realized that there were things in life that even teachers didn't understand.

Diverging Paths and All That

MARYANNE O'HARA

In Dollar Saver, the aisles are empty, customers crowding Electronics watching Nixon resign on twenty TV sets. Dad dropped us off with three bucks to buy burgers, but we've already spent it on fireballs and fudge.

While Nixon keeps the manager occupied, Billy demonstrates the "heads-up technique," the nonchalant gaze, his left hand filching Hershey bars and Bic pens while his right hand jingles pocket change. Billy grins, "I really save my dollars here."

Solo time. I head for Cosmetics, the wall of Peeper sticks—blue and green and lavender eye crayons that've always cost dollars I don't have. My hand closes around Seafoam Green, hesitates, but what the hell, even the President's a crook, so I slip it up my sleeve. I try to sneak away natural as Billy, but my legs move too quick and stiff.

Billy meets me in Electronics, where Nixon's keeping his head up, not admitting a damn thing. Saying he'd be able to clear his name if he fought long enough, but he'll sacrifice his honor for the country. When he says he'll resign as of noon the next day, I check out all these adults who yelled, "Impeach the crook." Nobody cheers. The faces are solemn as gravestones. Billy's motioning, Come on let's go, but suddenly I feel like I ate too much candy. I shake my sleeve, dropping the Peeper Stick onto a shelf, and follow Billy out the automatic doors. Dad's picking us up in two minutes, but Billy's headed someplace else.

A Whole Other

CARON A. LEVIS

It's like she got all her feelins and everythin already. For real.

I tell you that but you just be noddin like yeah, yeah. Like you know what I'm talkin bout even though you don't. And then you wilin bout the math quiz, askin me to fix your hoop where it got all caught up in your braid, an buggin bout your behind in my old jeans. An thas cool. I'll help you with your hoop, and shoot my mouth off bout how messed it is Ms. Hudson be quizzin us the day right after all those state tests, but girl I just got nothin bout you in those blue jeans right now. And in my mind I am havin a whole other conversation with you.

Cause I'm mad tired. Cause she don't sleep. And if she don't sleep nobody sleep cause that girl cryin's a hundred sirens blastin. In my mind I'm telling you thank god for these diapers that got Elmo's face on one side and his red fuzzy butt on the other, so you know which side goes where. Cause yesterday my mom decided once I get home from school, she's not helpin. I am the mom in charge of my daughter. Daughter. That word used to mean me. Says she wants me to learn for real this baby's mine. Like I don't know my own baby is my own baby when she came out of my own body, right? I mean thas crazy, right?

In my mind I'm askin you that.

But out loud I'm just sayin yeah, you be lookin tight in that new red hoodie.

Yeah, those sneakers fly.

In my mind I gotta admit to you my mom hit some truth for real. Cause even though that baby made me fat, kicked me from the inside, and came outta me in fronta my own eyes, sometimes I think if I catch some hours, she be gone when I wake up. Like she just some dream baby.

But first, I gotta remind you—quit shakin your behind in my face like you in some club when you in the hall, girl—no, I can't go with you to Nicole's party. Oh, yeah, you forgot. Duh.

Must be nice to forget about my baby.

Yeah I heard everybody's goin, and your boy Hector's gonna DJ. And yeah, probably Dondre might show up. Whatever. Not like I care.

But in my mind I'm telling you every day I be thinkin maybe he's gonna come ask to see her. But he don't. I mean, I know boys is weak like that, but I was hopin—

You stupid? No, I can't bring her to the party.

In my mind I'm tellin you how even though we sitting next to each other on this bench like we always do—it's like some big curtain be hangin between us. Same one they had between the hospital beds, so, even though you can hear me breathin, you don't know who I am behind here. Cause maybe I wanna be wishin we could still do it up how we used to do—but I just can't go there. Not if I'm gonna do her right.

Yeah you could wear my Peach Pocket skirt. No, it still don't fit. Yeah, fine—quit your beggin—keep it.

But I'm wishing you'd quit asking for my clothes. Like I'm dead or somethin.

Hey, remember how you kept singin Beyonce into my belly?

But you not hearin me. You wavin and shoutin to Melina

down the hall. So I don't bother askin if you remember when Dondre bailed on me last minute and mom couldn't get offa work, so you came to that crazy breathing class with me. Crackin me up with those faces, everybody shakin heads, callin us the giggle sisters. And then you got all quiet and said for real, don't freak out. Sayin we don't need no boys cause we got us and this lamazzawhateva's a snap. You got my back. Remember that? I kinda wish you'd quit dancin round and say that again.

Cause she had me up all night. She was cryin and I went in there, she's mad wet and—

What? No, I don't know why this gum always gotta lose flavor so quick. How my sposed to care bout the flavor-keeping of your gum when I'm tryin to tell you bout this whole other tiny person livin, sleepin, cryin, feelin, wantin in my house? How it's my job to give her all of everything. Cause I put her here. I'm her mom. So in the middle of last night when you dreamin bout Hector, I'm wiping, and rubbin in lotion, making sure Elmo's facing front so she stop screamin. Which she do.

In the middle of the night, my baby—Shine—she smiles. And I be her mom.

And she's so beautiful. And I can't breathe.

I try tellin you that part out loud—but you mouthin bout how you and Melina be applyin for that summer prep course that you know I can't do now.

What's your problem, flashin that in my face?

And you say like I care? All I be is baby this and baby that, actin all grown, like I'm too busy to bother with old stuff. But see you don't got a baby to sweat you all the time so you still carin bout homework, and parties, and havin a best friend, so excuse you if you gonna find Melina and get some lunch.

And you know—now that you be stalkin your way down the hall—I can see your behind do look superfine in those jeans.

Wish I told you that before. Cause now you too far away to hear. You can't hear me when I say it's true, I got my baby, and these worries, and those smiles, but you my best friend—that's a whole other thing.

And I still need you to keep me breathin.

The Burden of Agatha

NATALIE HANEY TILGHMAN

The year I make my Confirmation, sixth grade, Ms. Randolph is my Tuesday night CCD teacher. She wears twin sets and frosted lipstick. But the skin on her chin is sewed together in a way that makes the right side of her mouth dip into a bulldog's frown. And on top of that, her short hair reminds me of pencil shavings. The boys sing before she comes into class: "Be all that you can be in the Army." They think she fought in the Gulf War, that sand fleas bit her face and gave her the pink scar. Tom Smith, whose brother lost his arm in Iraq, says shrapnel from a bomb may have hit her. He says it cuts like broken glass and gets stuck inside the skin.

No one likes Ms. Randolph. She makes us memorize all of the Sacraments, the Disciples' names, the Act of Contrition, the Ten Commandments. We have to recite prayers out loud in the bored, monotone voices our parents use at Mass on Sunday. Sandra Smith cheats and writes the Apostles' Creed on her palm in purple pen so she can remember it. But when she rests her chin on her hand, the words transfer to the skin on her cheek like a disposable tattoo. Ms. Randolph makes her stand for the rest of the class, the same punishment she gave Matt Kellogg when he glued the books and pencils of some St. Patrick's student to the inside of the desk. We all thought what Matt Kellogg did was funny, but Ms. Randolph told us that Catholic day school kids are not like us publics. They are sensitive.

For Confirmation, we all get to pick a new middle name. Most of the girls want Elizabeth, Ann, Mary, Patricia. You have to choose a saint's name and if not, Ms. Randolph has to approve it. When Sandra Smith asks about Whitney, after Whitney Houston, Ms. Randolph says to see her after class. I choose Agatha so that my initials are NAP, a real word, instead of NSP. Also, Agatha Christie writes my favorite mystery books. I don't put these reasons on my request form. I just say I like St. Agatha.

A few weeks later, we read about the sacrament of marriage in our workbook. Matt Kellogg raises his hand, waving it wildly in the air. "You're not married, are you Ms. Randolph?" he asks with a smirk. He knows the answer. All of our married teachers go by missus. "Ms." is what is used for teachers who don't have husbands and the word buzzes like a mosquito in the ear.

The other boys snicker.

Someone whispers loudly, "Not with that face." Probably it is Tom Smith because he's gotten meaner since his brother came home from Iraq. We don't collect clothes and food for his family anymore.

The class erupts. Laughter rolls out in waves. I know it is mean, but I join in—we all do, even Mary Sue who wants to be a nun someday.

Ms. Randolph covers the scar with her hand. She sniffs loudly and leaves the room. A rush of wind flies in as the door closes behind her. On the wall, the crucifix flaps like a trapped bird.

A few minutes later, Sister Rose enters. Her habit is so tight that her eyebrows arch and almost touch her widow's peak. "You should be ashamed of yourselves." Sister's blue eyes, the color of a hot flame, survey the room. "In your Confirmation year, as you prepare to receive the Holy Spirit,

I am shocked to hear what was said to Ms. Randolph. Maybe some of you don't know. But I am sure others of you do, since it was in the paper just last year. I will remind you that Ms. Randolph was the victim of a horrible crime. And that a man attacked her in broad daylight." Sister Rose zeroes in on Matt Kellogg and roasts him with her eyes. "Those who said cruel things to Ms. Randolph know who you are. I want you all to bow your heads now and ask for forgiveness." She makes the sign of the cross and so do we. "Oh My God, I am sorry for my sins with all my heart . . . "

I squeeze my eyes shut and join the others in prayer. My mom didn't tell me what happened to Ms. Randolph, but I try to picture her running from a man wearing a mask. It is hard to imagine Ms. Randolph doing anything other than standing next to the overhead projector and leading us in the rosary.

After we say "Amen," Sister Rose hands back our Confirmation name request forms. On the top of mine, Ms. Randolph has written: "Agatha is a nice choice and my own Confirmation name. As you must know, St. Agatha underwent much suffering, including the mutilation of her breasts. You may have seen her on the stained glass windows in church carrying her breasts on a plate. She is the patron saint of rape victims." I want to change names after I read this, but it is too late. My mom has already ordered a gold monogrammed cross pendant for me.

No Boundaries

DAVID LLOYD

Kids who didn't like sports liked dodgeball because there weren't team captains, strategies, or special skills required. There was nothing to remember. All you did was throw a big rubber ball. If you hit someone, he's out. If he catches the ball, you're out. If he dodges, someone grabs it and the game goes on. I was bad at most sports: too small for basketball, too timid for football, too easily bored for baseball. But in dodgeball, the small and the timid survive. Surviving was all you did. It was like being in class when I hadn't done homework. I'd slump in the chair and squint my eyes so the teacher would look at me without seeing me, like you'd look at an ordinary cloud in a sky of clouds. Soon the bell would ring, and I'd survived another class.

* * *

After the coach split us into teams, he tossed a coin and handed the ball to the other side. The bravest moved forward when the coach blew the whistle. They shouted insults while small boys retreated to the back wall. Dodgeball could be vicious. Big kids used smaller ones as shields. Some targeted others because they were fat, quiet, or just unpopular. Once, a dodgeball slammed Mike Simmons's head so hard he blacked out.

For boys who weren't afraid, the beginning of dodgeball was as easy as stepping on ants: fifteen boys on each side, crowded together. The trick was to aim low, throw hard. My team's top shooter was Todd Rifkin, a basketball player with long arms and big hands. The best on the other side was Jay Palmer, the football team's quarterback. During the first ten minutes eight boys on my team and seven on the other team were hit. No one aimed at me, and I sidestepped misfired shots.

After twenty minutes only Todd, Jimmy Coleman, and I survived, with four boys on the other side. Jimmy and I hung by the back wall while Todd picked off three of our opponents. When he hit Harry Connors—our football team's fullback— a red welt puffed up on Harry's leg. But when Todd threw at Jay he aimed high, and Jay caught the ball against his chest.

"You're out!" the coach yelled.

So there was just Jimmy and me against the wall, and a smiling Jay Palmer with the ball. Jimmy and I kept apart and away from corners. When Jay walked to the line, he cocked his arm, focusing on me. But instead of me, he turned and popped Jimmy right on his head. Everyone—including the coach—laughed at that trick shot, which came so fast that Jimmy stood still for a while, wondering what happened. The ball hit the floor, and I grabbed it.

Jay backed up. I walked to the line, uncomfortable being the center of attention. The ball felt oversized and heavy. My teammates shouted encouragements: "You've got him! Nail him!" But I knew I didn't have him. As I drew my arm back, I thought that if Jay could catch a ball thrown by Todd, there was no hope for me. My toss sank to the floor three feet from Jay, and dribbled toward him. Laughter rippled around the gym. Jay's teammates began to shout, "Finish him off!" Jay jogged to the line as I backed away. He fired at my head, but I ducked. The ball slammed into the wall and bounced to Jay. He threw three quick shots, two I dodged by jumping left, one by ducking right. Each time the ball bounced back to Jay. His teammates stopped chanting, and I could see red blotches on Jay's forehead.

This was a new experience—inhabiting a body that moved quickly, gracefully. I felt weightless, like an astronaut jumping on the moon. I had become one of those flies you can't swat. You study it, wait your chance as it settles on the table, rubbing its back legs. You slam down your hand—but somehow it reappears, buzzing above your head. I was hovering against the back wall. I could detect the slightest realigning of Jay's arms and legs, gauge the ball's speed, and jump away just in time.

The coach blew his whistle and shouted, "No boundaries!" The order took a second to register with Jay, but soon he was grinning at me. Now he could hunt me anywhere, and circled left to force me to the right corner. I saw a chance to run behind him. But before I could, he fired at close range. The ball hit as if someone had punched me in the stomach. I fell backwards, pushed by the ball, my head slamming on the floor. I'd never felt such pain in my gut and head. Then I heard a noise around me and realized after a moment that it was my teammates cheering. I'd kept hold of the ball, cradled against my stomach.

"You all right?" the coach asked as boys filed to the locker room. "You got the wind knocked out of you."

I nodded.

"Okay. Time to go."

I thought that if I tried to get up, I'd pass out. The coach took the ball from me.

"Nice catch," he said. "If that game were a sport, you'd be a pro." He yanked me up by my hand.

I walked slowly to a bench in the locker room. I needed to sit until the throbbing in my stomach slowed.

Jay Palmer and Todd Rifkin were showered and dressed when they passed me on their way to the hall. Their wet hair was parted on the same side. Todd was saying something about Saturday night, and Jay nodded and turned his head, and his eyes met mine. I was sure he was going to say something. Maybe about the game, maybe something else. But then he turned back to Todd, laughed at words I couldn't hear, and they walked on through the door to the next class.

History

BETH ALVARADO

My mom had this box in the top of her closet where she kept old stuff, photos, letters, things like that. She called it the Box of the Past because she'd read this poem once where the guy said, "Whenever your name comes up, the box marked 1934 falls off the shelf." Isn't memory just like that, my mom said, somebody says one little thing—like "high school"—and everything comes tumbling out. Even if you don't want it to. You can't control it.

Songs, photographs, certain smells were like that for me.

I knew where the box was because whenever I wanted to see a picture of my real dad, my mom would get it down and show me. It was always the same picture: her and my dad, long hair, hippies, she was pregnant with me. Right before he left for college.

I never thought it was weird, how she only had *one*, until this day in American History when the teacher was talking about how we believe things are true because we've seen pictures, but then he said, someone had to make those pictures. Someone had to decide which details were important enough to write down. Someone had to decide what should be in a book and what should be left out. Just think, he said, if you were living in the South during the Civil War, you would think Lincoln was a tyrant. But what if the South had won? What if they had written the books? What would they have left out? History is a kind of fiction that way, he said, pictures can lie. You always have to ask yourself what was left out.

Now, I knew you could crop things out of a photograph, but it suddenly occurred to me that my mom could be leaving things out of the story altogether. How did I know she had only one picture of my dad? She'd never let me look in the box. No, she would take it down and show me one or two things. On my last birthday, for instance, she showed me a picture of her best friend, Amanda, who got killed in a car accident when they were sixteen, and then she gave me this silver ring that had belonged to her. At first, I felt kind of funny about the ring, like it was just the ring of some *dead* girl, you know, bad luck to wear it, maybe. So I wouldn't wear it. Instead, I hung it on a ribbon over a picture on my dresser. Then one night, when my mom saw it hanging there, she held it in her hand for a long time. She looked at it like it was so precious. And a part of me thought—I couldn't help it—a part of me thought I would have to *die* for her to feel that way about me.

Anyways, that day in class, I decided to look in the box for myself, to see what she had left out, was saving for later, or maybe was never going to tell me. I had a right to know. After all, her history was my history. Maybe there were lots of pictures of my dad in there. Maybe even letters. Maybe one explaining why he never came back. Maybe an address.

When I opened the box, I felt like I was on the brink of discovery, but she kept such random stuff. If you were an archeologist, what would you make of shells and beach glass? I guessed you'd figure she liked the ocean. There were a lot of photos of her and Amanda. Amanda looked like she could've been one of my friends and it was weird to think that now she should be nearly as old as my mom, but, instead, she looked like me. Amanda would never get any older. She'd always be a teenager. I'd never thought about death, how it freezes you in time, but there it was. In three years, I'd be older than Amanda ever was.

And then there were other things: postcards, ticket stubs. Photos of my mom standing with some guy, his arm around her. None of me. Which kind of took my breath away. Not one. Didn't I count? Or if I went further down through the layers, none of my grandma. None of my mom's childhood. There were some of her with the other half of the picture cut away. Or in a dress with some guy, but she'd burned a hole where his face was supposed to be. My dad, I guessed.

So this is what it all meant: there were important things she wasn't telling me. What? She didn't trust me? And so I wondered, Would she ever include me? Or, like she did with my grandma, would she leave me out of the box forever? Or could she, one day, get so mad at me that she'd burn a hole where my face was supposed to be? Erase me. Never tell stories. Never look back.

Even when I was little, I felt like she was fragile, like I had to protect her. Even when I was little, I would do anything to make her look at me, really look. To make her laugh. To keep her happy. To keep from being invisible. But it hadn't worked and now, now, maybe that was why I liked to make her mad. I felt like I had to dig, to hurt her to get inside.

Open up, Mom, I wanted to say, let me in.

And I actually saw myself like a heart surgeon, my hands wrenching open her rib cage. I saw her bloody heart, and still, I didn't know her. So this is what I did, I left her a note. It said: *I belong in here. If this is your history, where am I? I don't see one baby picture. Not one lock of hair. No baby shoes. Nothing.*

The Coat

LEX WILLIFORD

Eighth grade. Mrs. Jaffrey's class. It was always cold in Mrs. Jaffrey's class. It was always freezing in there. And every day I wore my coat to her class she told me not to.

"Why not?" I asked her. "It's cold in here. I'm cold."

"Because you're not supposed to wear your coat to class," she kept saying.

Seemed pretty stupid to me, so I kept wearing my coat to class. I was cold.

After a few days, Mrs. Jaffrey told me to hang my coat up in the principal's office. Told me to stay there for the rest of the afternoon. Told me to write her a five-hundred word essay on why I shouldn't wear my coat to class.

"Why?" I asked her. "I can't do that. How'm I supposed to do that?"

She looked at me over her horn-rims. Her lips were white. She had her arms folded. The north wind coming up off the practice fields outside had glazed the windowpanes along the wall with ice.

"Be creative," she said.

I sat in the principal's warm office and wrote a hundred sentences, like the ones I'd written on the detention hall chalkboard for Mrs. Jaffrey after school:

I will not wear my coat to class because someone might mistake me for a bear and shoot me.

I will not wear my coat to class because I might sweat so much the class will flood, and somebody might drown.

I will not wear my coat to class because I might get so hot I'll catch fire and burn the whole junior high down.

That kind of thing. It was more than five hundred words. I thought it was pretty creative.

Mrs. Jaffrey didn't think so, though. Neither did my old man. Next day, he showed up outside Mrs. Jaffrey's class with my essay in his hand. Checked me out of school. Told me to put on my coat.

"It's in the principal's office," I told him.

"Leave it, then," he said.

It was cold outside. Ice coated the trees, the rooftops of houses, the windshields of cars parked along the curbs, the sidewalks, the streets. My father drove too fast, dodging fallen tree limbs in the road, his pickup truck sliding all over, down to Pecan Park. He told me to get out. Told me to open the tailgate. Told me to set the essay there on the tailgate in front of me. Told me to bend over and read each sentence, one at a time.

There was a new two-by-four in the bed of the truck. The wood was white. He picked it up, stood behind me. I read a sentence, and then he hit me one. Then I read another sentence. He hit me again. There were a hundred sentences. He kept hitting me. The wind blew up hard and it started to sleet, and all around the park tree limbs groaned and creaked and snapped off. I didn't have my coat on. I was cold. Ice fell all around me.

Raised by Wolves

CRAIG MORGAN TEICHER

He could have been, though he was not. He had never even seen a wolf—he had lived with his father and mother in a big white house with a bay window. But, had he been left in the woods—though they would never have left him anywhere, and never went in the woods—wolves could have found him, and instead of thrashing him about until he was only something for them to eat, they could have taken him in as one of their own, though, of course, this is not what happened.

Though had it happened, he would never have had to suffer his father's senseless midnight rages, nor his anxious morning silence, as though the day had been haunting him all night long, nor his mother's cowed protectiveness, all of which he did suffer, swaddled in a silence of his own. But he could have learned to detect the unfamiliar scent of an intruder in the woods, or the well-known odor of an enemy. He could have known how to distinguish predator from prey by the rustling of the leaves. Though what would prey on a wolf?

Of course, he never had to answer that question, for he was safe in his house, where even the walls cast shadows and the floors groaned to mark the slow passing of his long childhood years.

But he could have run with the pack—perhaps he could have even led it, were he able to tame his fellow wolves by filling their hearts with fear, which they deeply love, for fear brings order to their wild lives, tells them where to go and what to do. For he did know that those whom he most feared, and those whom he tried to make most afraid, were the ones whose love he most deeply needed.

Trapped

SHELBY RAEBECK

Shooting hoops at the court behind the Presbyterian church, I noticed an old blue Taurus wagon, and inside, a dark figure watching. A few days later, the same car pulled in and Lance Williams, the star of the high school team who lived in Freetown, North Hampton's black section, got out.

"I heard about some backwards-dunking white boy," he said.

We chose for the ball and played dead even until point game, when Lance backed me toward the basket, then stepped back and drained a jump shot before I could even leave my feet.

"Good game," he said.

"Yeah," I said, slapping his hand.

He walked through the gate, the back of his shirt dark with sweat, then turned back, looking through the chain-link fence.

"I've seen you in school," he said. "You don't say much."

"Guess not," I said.

"Well," he said, "maybe there ain't nothing *to* say." And he walked off to his car.

In school, Lance talked me into going out for the team, and two weeks later we were matched up in scrimmages, both of us 6'2", him the star, me the newcomer, the only other kid with skills and above-the-rim hops. After he scored on me, he'd say,

"Aw, come on now." Then I'd bust him back, and he'd smile and wink. "Yeah," he'd say, "that fire starting to come out."

We won our first game, Lance scoring twenty, me nineteen, and afterward I rode with Lance, leaving my bike chained to the rack, and we cruised Main Street, then drove the long loop, hitting all the beaches on the bay side before swinging over to the ones on the ocean. Not even mentioning the game, Lance just wanted to drive, from beach to beach. By the time we got pulled over, I was nearly asleep.

"What's going on, officer?" Lance said rolling down his window.

"Where you fellas headed?" the cop said.

"Just driving," Lance said.

"Where to?"

"Nowhere," Lance said.

"You been drinking?"

"Did I do something wrong?"

"Routine check."

"My ass," Lance muttered.

"What's that?" The cop leaned in the window.

I thought it might help if the cop saw me, and I leaned over. "We had a game tonight," I said.

The cop looked from me back to Lance. "Guess you just never learned your manners," he said, and returned to his cruiser.

We pulled in the first driveway after the Freetown trailer park, beside a small, shingled house, and Lance shut off the motor.

"You believe that cop?" he said.

"Trying to break the boredom," I said.

"It ain't boredom, Ricky."

"Whatever." I opened the door, ready to go inside.

"If that's how you feel, okay," Lance said. "But don't come over my house and tell me the dude is pulling me over, telling me mind my manners because he's bored."

I pulled my door closed and sat there watching our breath fog the windshield, feeling like I'd been pulled into a trap.

"So what's this 'breaking the boredom'?" Lance said.

"He's just some cop with nothing better to do than mess with a couple of high school kids."

"He wasn't messing with you, Ricky."

I didn't respond, just sat there, the windows completely fogged, wondering how long it would take to walk home.

"You gonna say anything?" Lance said finally.

"Sometimes," I said, "there ain't nothing *to* say."

The next day at practice Lance and I kept our distance. Then, when we scrimmaged, I caught an outlet pass and angled toward the basket, only Lance having a chance to stop me. Sensing an edge, I figured what the hell, cocked the ball in my right hand as I leaped, and slammed it down through the hoop.

Only once I'd landed and turned to run back up the court did I see where Lance had stopped a few feet short of the basket, never even bothering to jump. And though I was pumped from throwing it down off a dead run, the thrill was cheapened by Lance just letting me go.

"Nice effort," I said, trotting back up court.

"What's that?" Lance said, catching up to me, both of us stopping and facing each other.

"You just gave up," I said.

"It's a scrimmage," he said. "Who gives a shit?"

Coach called us from the other end of the court.

"So just forget it, right?" I said to Lance. "Forget everything."

"Right," he said.

"'Cause your shit is too thick to crawl out of," I said, the words surprising me.

His body tightened, shoulders straightening, and he stepped up close, bringing his face to within a few inches of mine. I didn't back up, just stared into his hardened eyes.

"It's true," I said, words coming I'd never even thought. "You're stuck in your own shit."

Lance swung quickly, his fist connecting with the bridge of my nose, sending me reeling back. I straightened up and blinked to clear my eyes.

"And now," I said, "you're a nigger throwing punches."

Lance swung again but this time I ducked, and before he could get off another punch the other players had reached us, two of them holding him back.

Coach asked us who had started it and we both said simultaneously, "He did."

Then, looking at Lance, thinking back over the last two months, back to when he walked out on the court behind the church, I decided he was right. He may have sought me out, and drawn me in, but the words I spoke were all mine.

"I did," I said to Coach, then looked at Lance. "You happy now?" I said.

"Yeah," he said, and turned and walked away. Then he stopped and turned back. "So you do have something to say," he said.

But I just stood there looking at him, saying nothing, watching him turn again and walk off across the gym, the expanse between us widening, the curve of the earth swelling up between us into the hard shining floor.

Thud

NAOMI SHIHAB NYE

There are many things Rainey does not understand: war, and running with the bulls, for two examples. Why get anywhere near herds of bulls and irritate them in the first place? Why is this popular? She would prefer to be liked by bulls—to meet them in a placid zone and stare at one another, trade some secrets, if possible.

She has no desire to binge-drink or congregate with believers. The pious confidence of people who think they know "the truth" repels her. If only one could slap them with mysteries. . . .

She pictures herself on the edge of any scene.

Scenes need fringe observers—people to take notes and tell what you did later.

If you can find them.

The episodes seemed so tiresome—who liked whom, who had broken up, or overdosed—flickering hordes of rumors—she abandoned them all. A wide swath of her brain felt relieved. She had no interest in Adderall. She made up a boyfriend named Leo who lived in Wisconsin, where no one she knew had been. His parents were professors who stayed home by the fireplace reading all winter long.

At school, if someone asked her to do something sociable, she'd say, "I'm okay." If pressed, she'd say something about Leo. They were working on a long-distance project. Something, anything.

On weekends, Rainey pitched a book and water bottle into her basket and rode her bicycle around the abandoned brewery and the ancient mill. One day, the waterwheel was spinning again. She watched parents prepare birthday parties for their kids at Roosevelt Park, hanging piñatas, weighting paper tablecloths down with horrible giant soda bottles. She conversed with abandoned dogs and dreamed of delivering them all to the Utopia Animal Sanctuary where they would be cared for with kindness and attention.

Rainey felt she needed to examine the mysteries of her childhood years more deeply before going off to college. Those weird reverberations around the sixth grade year, what was that all about? That sense of precipice—as if you'd gone hiking and reached a cliff at the end of the trail and where was your parachute? Because the days were definitely, definitely going to push you off. And if you hadn't learned rock-climbing by then, or discovered some way to bungee jump, you were in big trouble. Rainey had never yet fully reckoned with the sixth grade. Was she still standing there, immobilized? Had everyone jumped but her?

This was not something you could talk about with the homecoming queen.

Mostly, she was still stunned by the shock of her father's death, when she was a freshman and he was still a relatively young man who had a heart attack after work one day. Strangers called 911 when they saw him slumped against his car in the bank parking lot. He'd been taken to hospital, and was "well on the road to recovery," said the doctor to Rainey's mother, a few days later, the day he died.

Rainey had taken a bus to the hospital right after school, carrying a small tub of *tabooleh,* her father's favorite salad. She had a frozen blue ice pack in the pocket of her schoolbag.

Outside her father's room, she was stunned to be hugged hard by a woman she'd never seen before. A black nurse with an open face wearing a print smock—small yellow bears holding balloons, Rainey recalled later. Who was she?

"He didn't make it, honey. Oh honey, he's just left us." The nurse had stifled a sob.

Was she selected for her softness, her resonant voice? The official hugger-nurse who stood outside stricken rooms to greet the first people who showed up, alert them that they were at a new cliff? Surely, that must be a weird position to apply for. Professional hard-times hugger.

Rainey wondered some days, if she went to the hospital again, could she find the woman? Could she ask more questions—like, did he call out when he died, did someone hear him, or was it simply the monitor which began moaning its loud alert, what exactly happened? I'm ready to hear it now, please. Could Rainey tell her, he'll never leave me, just wanted to let you know?

Both Rainey and her mother felt horribly guilty that they had not been at his bedside when he died. Rainey's mother had been back at work—she thought he was stable and soon to be released. Apparently people commonly died when their loved ones were out of the room. Bathroom break. Quick trip down to cafeteria for a grilled cheese. It was easier to die if you didn't have family members to worry about at that exact moment.

Easier for the one who was dying, maybe.

Rainey kept wondering what she would have done had she been there, with her dad. Who expected anyone to have a second heart attack on top of a first? She would not eat *tabooleh* again until she was twenty-three.

Did his sudden departure have anything to do with her inability to negotiate the social roller coaster now?

Then a bird flew into the window of English Literature during discussion of Gerard Manley Hopkins. Someone tittered. After class Rainey went outside. A gray mourning dove, stunned on the ground. Rainey filled the cap of her water bottle, poured water over the bird's beak. The beak opened a tiny bit. The bird opened an eye.

A boy knelt down beside her. "Hey," he said. "Sad bird. I'm Leo."

The Pillory

PAUL LISICKY

A replica of a pillory in a replica of a Colonial town. My right arm into the right hole, my left arm into the left. My neck went right through the center. I laughed, not because there was anything remotely funny about being hung up in a cross, but just because it felt good to be away from home, school. The marketplace steamed with activity. The worn patch of grass beside the horseblock, the boxwoods by the cobbler's shop, the flies buzzing above the tidy piles of dung. And it wasn't any wonder that the faces before me receded in the glare. It wasn't any wonder that I stopped thinking of my mother and her neck aches or my father and his call for constant motion whenever he was home from work, even though we never got anything done. I was giving the wood exactly what it wanted. No one was going anywhere. And it was a relief to admit to what was what.

I didn't think of the other boys once punished like that. I didn't give a thought to the eggs, fruit, mice, and shit thrown at their faces. *There can be no outrage more flagrant,* Hawthorne said, *than to forbid the culprit to hide his face for shame.* But was it shame I felt? I only knew that I was tired of holding myself up. I wanted to cave in and so I caved in. Which was why, after I'd grown used to my new position, I pulled myself out and forgot I had a body.

Or took three steps backward and fell a hard five feet to the ground.

It wasn't me, then, that dropped like a bale of hay from a burning barn. It wasn't me lying on my back as the crowd looked on. Or me, for that matter, covering my crotch with my hand, as if I'd already known that they were hungry for murder.

A little girl screamed, and I was relieved to hear that scream tear through the heat.

Relieved, too, to hear my father walking out of the crowd. Relieved to see the arm he raised, for wasn't that him reaching out to help me up? No, that was the crowd in that arm—I can only see it from here—and he was setting his face for what he didn't want to do, which was to spank me as one spanks an errant child, not a twelve-year-old boy whose voice was on the verge of changing.

Once, twice: Who can remember such things? Did I feel it? Did I send myself away? He hit me as the crowd looked on, even as his eyes said, Who am I doing this for? Aren't you my son? He stopped and he blinked, as if he hadn't known where he'd gone. Then led me to a tool shed on the periphery, where he cleaned off my knee with a handkerchief he'd pulled from his pocket.

I spent the rest of the day swimming back and forth across the motel pool until the chlorine stung. I got up. I got up in the way we all get up against the arm that wants to keep us down.

Maybe that's what my father already knew back then. And maybe that's why he brought it up at the dinner table thirty years later, though I'd forgotten it, as I'd forgotten many things by then. His eyes looked through me, past me. He spoke as if that memory were just one more thing he'd been wearing around his neck, and the straight-ahead gaze it required of him was no longer serving him at this late hour, what with the bills stacking up on his desk, my mother in Ranmar Gardens, and the empty rooms of the apartment that needed cleaning.

Which was why I didn't throw the balled-up napkin in my hand, though I'd be lying if I didn't admit to that temptation. I put my hand over my father's. And looked away from the face that didn't need my forgiveness.

Theology

THOMAS JEFFREY VASSEUR

I.

My cousin Theo hung on for three months, so when my
mother told me yesterday, I just couldn't believe it. Why
only last summer Theo and I smoked grapevines in our
fort by the creek, talked about girls, played flashlight tag in
granddaddy's cornfield, then we showed off the body hair
we'd grown since Christmas. It used to be divine. Almost
every holiday, Theo and his parents would drive down from
Springfield and we would catch up on everything, think
up new pranks to pull on his older brother, tell wild stories
lying in our bunk beds until two or three in the morning—
or my father came with his belt. So if Aunt Elizabeth tries
to make me look in the casket, I'll tell her to leave me alone,
to just stop and think for once in her life. Besides, one memory's bad enough. I'm thirteen years old. I'll never forget it.
His chest crushed. Eyes like someone else's. After the accident Theo looked like a grown man, someone who weighed
two hundred pounds because of all the swelling. Lilac-
white blotched face. Dark violet bruises on his neck. When
I leaned over the hospital bed, though, he had grinned like
we had stolen a few beers, snuck off with an armful of my
brother's magazines, and climbed the mimosa in our backyard. When he saw my eyes water up, he grinned even wider
and whispered: "Hello there, squirrel." No one else was hurt.
The car Theo was in slid on some gravel going around a

curve, dropped off an embankment, then rolled over twice. On a Sunday, too! He'd appreciate that. The doctors said it was a miracle. Theo had survived after being thrown halfway through the sunroof, so I felt very lucky and made several silent promises to myself. I promised to do anything, anything if Theo would live, and to devote myself to some worthy task. I remembered to ask and it shall be given and to believe with all my heart.

II.

Sometimes when Theo visited Kentucky we would all go to church together, and whenever he came the strangest things would happen. One time in the middle of Easter service, the preacher opened his mouth and a wasp flew down his throat. Brother Sailor went into some kind of shock. His throat swelled shut and he would have asphyxiated and died if a registered nurse hadn't been right on hand to cut a little hole in it for him. But that's not all. A couple of summers later, the same preacher stood up before our congregation and announced that he was leaving the ministry. He said he was truly sorry. Then he started down the aisle, against the left side of the sanctuary, and kept on walking straight out the door. Theo and I liked Brother Sailor very much and were sort of sad to see him go. On Saturday afternoons, he played basketball with us. Once, he had even beaten Theo in this really intense watermelon-eating contest. The man had our respect! He always preached our favorite sermon on the hottest day of the year, the first week in July usually. That's when Theo's family would drive down with a trunk full of fireworks, contraband from across the Ohio River. The sermon went on and on, even had a title I'll never forget: "Ten Things to Do If You're Going to Hell." "Well, the first thing I'd do," Brother Sailor would say, "is to drink a taaaaall glass of iiice-cooooold water." He was from even farther south and those Arkansas vowels really tickled Theo. Whenever Brother Sailor got to that part about the ice water it just about killed us both.

III.
We would snicker and fidget and kick each other in the shins. Back then we could hardly sit still in the pews. But when the preacher apologized before our congregation that summery-sticky afternoon, a lot of other people had the same problem. Everybody looked shocked but fidgety. They all stayed put in their seats, twisting and turning to watch him walk out the door. Then they turned back around and began staring at the empty pulpit, gaping and gawking—at a real loss for words—all except Theo, who observed how the Lord sure moves in mysterious ways. I thought Aunt Elizabeth was going to whack him a good one, then and there, but the head of the deacons boomed out an "Amen!" He seemed to agree with Theo for some reason. Who knows what that old geezer was thinking? Outside in the car, we rejoiced some more. This meant we could go swimming, light some firecrackers, and ride the horses sooner, when out of the blue Theo piped up again: "I bet he's run away with the organist!" Well, that's all it took. Aunt Elizabeth starting screaming. She turned beet-red and slapped Theo across the face. Made his lip bleed. She told him to act right. She said that he'd had it coming for a long long time, and we had no business blaspheming and making fun of the pastor. After we got home, though, and had just finished dinner, our aunt's Sunday school teacher called up and said that's just what had happened. Brother Sailor and the organist were leaving town! The deacons were calling an emergency meeting! You can just imagine

all the commotion. I was screwing around outside, in our little orchard, trying to knock down some green apples using bottle rockets. Theo had gotten a good look at Aunt Elizabeth's face and he'd heard a little of the conversation coming through the receiver. When he came outside and told me, we both couldn't believe it. I thought we would never stop laughing.

Pep Assembly at Evergreen Junior High

DAVID PARTENHEIMER

A pep assembly was my only good experience in junior high. It may not sound like much of a memory unless you understand the situation. Even before I got to Evergreen Junior High School I heard tales from other kids about daily fights and weekly knifings. I shuddered with fear the whole summer, just thinking about the violence. I asked my father about junior high. He said he enjoyed the fights but avoided the knifings, and told me not to be a pansy. He bought two pairs of boxing gloves and taught me the stances and punches so that I could win the upcoming fights. He even mounted a punching bag in our basement for practicing the straight, hook, and uppercut punches. I pummeled the bag to a pulp, but I still felt unprepared for Evergreen Junior High.

On the first day, I rode my bicycle to school. I was the only kid to do so. No one told me it was uncool. However, a hulking boy pointed it out to me as I parked my bike in an empty rack. "What have you got there, wimp?" It was a dumb question but worthy of deference coming from the mouth of a burly brute twice my size. The Neanderthal pricked his ears for the slightest excuse to pummel me. I remounted my bicycle, rode it home, and jogged back. I was late, sent to the office, scolded, but alive on my first day at Evergreen Junior High.

However, my discretion did not spare me for long. It was a school ritual for the older boys to initiate the younger ones.

Do you understand the concept of initiating by intimidation, humiliation, and a good pounding? Three boys in my neighborhood understood the practice well. As you might recall, I was on foot so I walked right into their ambush. All three wanted to fight me at the same time. They were stumbling over each other for first rights. I resolved their conundrum by challenging the smallest one to a fistfight with boxing gloves. They were befuddled at the notion but could not think of any reason not to pick up the gauntlet. The four of us headed to my house to get the gloves. I could have taken refuge inside my room instead of bringing out the gloves, but the bullies would have pounded me even worse the next day for tricking them. So I fought in single combat on my front lawn. As it turned out, my father had taught me well. I was surprised how much a human head and a punching bag have in common. When I bloodied the guy's nose with a hook and loosened a few of his teeth with a straight punch, the gang left and never bothered me again. They were hoodlums of honor.

Well, I think you have enough sense of situation. You are now ready for the pep assembly. Imagine the perverted mind that thinks adolescent boys and girls need pep. Nonetheless, we marched out of class single file and assembled in the auditorium to cheer on our varsity basketball team. On stage, some cheerleaders performed flips and cartwheels around the team while others beat on tambourines and blew on whistles. In step to the commotion, the varsity boys strutted about the stage, shaking their fists above their heads and roaring their devotion to the team. In hot pursuit, the cheerleaders wiggled their short pleated skirts, jiggled their pompoms, then fell to the ground in splits for us all to see. I must confess I enjoyed this part and it pepped me up considerably. The entire student body was pepped up and shouted in unison, "Go team go! Evergreen Eagles score! Go team go!"

At this moment, the principal popped up on stage to announce a musical interlude. I would have preferred another round of the cheerleaders doing splits. I expected the usual off-key medley from the marching band or a fervent rendition of the school song by the school chorus. Instead, a boy my age appeared on stage with a guitar strapped across his shoulder. The students grumbled, grunted, and groaned until the boy struck the first chord and sang the first verse of an unknown song. All the students in the audience and on stage fell still and silent. Their faces were frozen in the act of chewing gum, sticking out their tongues, blowing raspberries, or merely gawking in bewilderment.

I heard something beautiful during my first week at Evergreen Junior High. A boy like me was able to pick out a melody on a guitar and sing a song of his own about his soul breaking free of the muck and mire of this world and soaring free like a real eagle, not our school mascot. I wanted to become like him. I wanted a talent. I wanted to make music and live in my own world of beauty. I wished the moment would remain. But some goofball broke the trance when he woke up from his nap and started cussing. The cheerleaders snapped out of their stupor and threw their pompoms at the musician. They screamed and shouted at him, "Score, score, score!" Without a word, the boy left the stage. The cheerleaders beat their tambourines and blew their whistles. As a grand finale, the student body chanted the three words of the team song in unison: "Evergreen eagles soar! Evergreen eagles soar!"

But even above the din, I could still hear the voice of the boy singing.

My Brother at the Canadian Border

SHOLEH WOLPÉ

For Omid

On their way to Canada in a red Mazda, my brother and his friend, college freshmen with little sense, stopped at the border, and the guard leaned forward, asked: *Where you boys heading?*

My brother, *Welcome to Canada* poster in his eyes, replied: *Mexico.* The guard blinked, stepped back then forward, said: *Sir, this is the Canadian border.* My brother turned to his friend, grabbed the map from his hands, slammed it on his shaved head. *You stupid idiot*, he yelled, *you've been holding the map upside down.*

In the interrogation room full of metal desks and chairs with wheels that squeaked and fluorescent light humming, bombarded with questions, and finally: *Race?*

Stymied, my brother confessed: *I really don't know, my parents never said.* The woman behind the desk widened her blue eyes to take in my brother's olive skin, hazel eyes, the blond fur that covered his arms and legs. Disappearing behind a plastic partition, she returned with a dusty book, thick as *War and Peace.*

This will tell us your race. Where was your father born? she asked, putting on her horn-rimmed glasses.

Persia, he said.

Do you mean I-ran?

I ran, you ran, we all ran. He smiled.

Where's your mother from? Voice cold as a gun.

Russia, he replied.

She put one finger on a word above a chart in the book, the other on a word at the bottom of the page, brought them together looking like a mad mathematician bent on solving the crimes of zero times zero divided by one. Her fingers stopped on a word. Declared: *You are white.*

My brother stumbled back, a hand on his chest, eyes wide, mouth in an O as in *O my God! All these years and I did not know.* Then to the room, to the woman, and to the guards: *I am white. I can go anywhere. Do anything. I can go to Canada and pretend it's Mexico. At last, I am white and you have no reason to keep me here.*

The Engines of Sodom

JONATHAN PAPERNICK

Hershlag's mother hit him over the head with a loaf of rye bread when he told her he was going to catch a show at Ildiko's instead of joining her at synagogue to mark his grandfather's *yahrzeit*. "What's the matter with you? Poppa's been gone a year today and you're running downtown to fill your ears with that trash."

Hershlag raised a delicate middle finger, jumped on his skateboard, and wobbled down the driveway.

Connor and McManus were crouched on their boards in front of the club sharing a sodden pizza sub when Hershlag rolled up. They had large black X's drawn in marker on the backs of their hands and Hershlag was glad that he had had the foresight to mark himself before his mother went crazy.

In Hebrew school, he had been called Hershlag the Fag by the spoiled Forest Hill JAPs because he had acne and wore Lee, instead of Levi's; the next year, he was a skinhead boozing with Eamon Sturtze and Little John at the Bulldog. Now he didn't drink or smoke and hadn't been to the Bulldog since it had been shuttered following a bloody after-hours brawl.

He wore his high-top sneakers, an oversized *Walk Together, Rock Together* T-shirt and sanctimonious black X's scrawled onto his skin. "Gonna be a great show tonight, guys. I read in *Maximumrocknroll* that this band shreds."

"You haven't heard them?" McManus sneered.

"Sure I have. Their old stuff."

McManus rolled his eyes at Connor. "What's up with your arms, Hershlag?"

He hadn't had time to throw on long sleeves before his mother chased him out, and now his slim, scarred arms were visible for his new friends to see. It looked like a melon baller had scooped out the tender flesh of his forearms, leaving the wounds to heal into cruel putty-like scars.

"Got rid of some old tattoos," Hershlag said. "Dragons and skulls. Kids' stuff. I'm thinking of getting some new ones, though. You know, a little bit straight and a little bit edgy." He laughed, but his companions did not.

"Hey kids, don't forget your fake IDs," he quipped, trailing after them.

When old man Ildiko introduced the opening band, the club was already smoke-filled and packed. Hershlag popped in his earplugs and yelled something to McManus, who was talking up a dreadlocked Asian girl who lived in Kensington Market.

McManus spun around and poked Hershlag in the chest with a stiff finger. "Go away, Hershlag."

Connor scolded McManus and told him not to be so hard on the kid, then disappeared into the rolling wave of bodies.

Amid the clash of distorted buzzsaw guitars, Hershlag thought of his grandfather. Not long before he died, Poppa had approached Hershlag's bedroom. The music was blasting.

"Oy!" Poppa Hershlag had shouted. "Like the very engines of Sodom. Turn that racket off, Adam. It will put me in the ground."

Hershlag had laughed at how weak his grandfather's plaintive "Oy" sounded compared to the militant, testosterone-fueled Oi, oi, oi's chanted on his record.

Then Poppa Hershlag had seen the tattoos and shaken

his numbered arm at his only grandson. "Do you think this is a joke? Does this mean nothing to you? You are a lucky boy, Adam, to be born in the time you were born. Don't ever forget that."

Hershlag's scars itched and he scratched absently at them as the band cleared the stage.

Despite the swelling crowd pressing around him, Hershlag felt a deep loneliness and shame. He missed his grandfather and had done nothing to honor his memory. Poppa Hershlag deserved more than a candle and a muttered prayer.

Connor stumbled up from the mosh pit, sweating through his T-shirt. "I'm going backstage to hang with the band. Wanna come?"

Hershlag nodded and followed Connor through the crowd, but he was stopped by a voice calling, "Look who's back from the dead."

"And with the straight edge crew," a second voice added.

Eamon and Little John stood before Hershlag and Connor in identical oxblood Doc Marten boots, blue jeans, and red suspenders snapped tight over their Fred Perry polo shirts. They were a couple years older than Hershlag and towered over him like fully grown men.

Eamon flicked Hershlag in the nose with a battered finger. Eamon's head was newly shaved and a droplet of red blood had dried on the side of his scalp. "I didn't think I'd see your sorry ass again. What happened to your tats? I thought we were brothers." Then he gestured toward the swastika tattoo on his own forearm, the Death's Head, the SS lightning bolts.

The next band was doing its sound check and Connor had to shout to Hershlag. "You're a Nazi?"

"No, I'm not."

"He's a Jew. How can you miss a nose like that?" Eamon taunted.

Connor shook his blond head and burst through the crowd, shouting in disgust, "A Nazi."

"Oops," Eamon laughed and grabbed Hershlag's skateboard. "I guess you're out of friends, mate."

Hershlag stood a moment, trying to find the right words, but he was afraid that he would cry in front of Eamon and Little John, and nothing—nothing in the world, he was sure—could be worse than that. In an instant, he was running down Bloor Street, in search of the tattoo parlor, giant snot bubbles bursting from his nose. He had his grandfather's blurred blue numbers committed to memory and he was determined to become a living monument to Poppa Hershlag so that Hershlag himself would never forget.

The Barbie Birthday

ALISON TOWNSEND

Girls learn how to be women not from their dolls but from the women around them.
        Yona Zeldis McDonough, *The Barbie Chronicles*

The first gift my father's girlfriend gave me was the Barbie I wanted. Not the original—blond, ponytailed Barbie in her zebra-striped swimsuits and matching cat-eye shades— but a bubble-cut brunette, her hair a color the box described as "Titian," a brownish-orange I've never seen since. But I didn't care. My hair was brown too. And Barbie was Barbie, the same impossible body when you stripped off her suit, peeling it down over those breasts without nipples, then pulling it back up again. Which was the whole point, of course.

There must have been a cake. And ten candles. And singing. But what I remember is how my future stepmother stepped from the car and into the house, her auburn curls bouncing in the early May light, her suit of fuchsia wool blooming like some exotic flower, just that, then Barbie— whom I crept away with afterwards, stealing upstairs to play with her beneath a sunny window in what had been my parents' bedroom.

She likes me; she really likes me, I thought, recalling Shirley's smile when I opened the package. As I lifted the lid of Barbie's narrow, coffin-like box, she stared up at me, sloe-eyed, lids bruised blue, lashes caked thick with mascara, her mouth stuck in a pout both seductive and sullen. Alone, I turned her over and over in my hands, marveling at her stiff, shiny body— the torpedo breasts, the wasp waist, the tall-drink-of-water legs that didn't bend, and the feet on perpetual tiptoe, their arches crimped to fit her spike-heeled mules as she strutted across the sunny windowsill.

All Barbie had to do was glance back once and I followed, casting my lot with every girl on every block in America, signing on for life. She was who I wanted to be, though I couldn't have said then, anymore than I could have said that Barbie was sex without sex. I don't think my stepmother-to-be knew that either, just that she wanted to please me, the eldest daughter who remembered too much and who had been too shy to visit. My mother had been dead five months, both her breasts cut off like raw meat. But I yearned for the doll she'd forbidden, as if Barbie could tell me what everything meant— how to be a woman when I was a girl with no mother, how to dress and talk, how to thank Shirley for the hard, plastic body that warmed when I touched it, leading me back to the world.

The Last Good Night

TODD JAMES PIERCE

When I was young, my brother was my best friend, my teacher. He showed me how to ride a bike without training wheels and how to catch a ball in a fielder's mitt. The year I was unpopular at school, he taught me how to protect myself in a playground fight. Hold your fists like this, he said.

Like this? I asked.

He took my hands in his. No, he said. Like *this*.

When I was old enough, he introduced me to basketball, which had been our father's favorite sport. He showed me the best way to shoot, demonstrating the movements repeatedly until I understood the subtle actions that made up the game. The secret to dribbling, he said, was sensing the ball's position. Keep your eyes on your opponent, not the ball. He showed me how to play man-on-man defense, how to set a screen and make a hook shot. He said basketball was the most interesting game a person could know. He looked at the space between us, as though his words hovered there. Because of this, I understood it was something our father had told him once, in those months before he left us for good.

During each game, my mother and I watched my brother play, amazed at his ability. Even though he was only five-feet-ten, he could still step through air and slam the ball home. He could fake a drive then put such a sweet spin on an outside shot that the ball almost always found the hoop. When he stood at the free-throw line, his shots never touched the rim: they passed smoothly through the orange hoop, checked only by the net before falling to the ground.

Three times that year, his picture appeared in the local paper—my brother mid-air, the ball cradled in his hand. We cut them out, stuck them to our refrigerator. But there was something else: after each appearance, for days, my brother checked the mailbox, hoping there might be a letter for him.

Our streak of good luck lasted only nine months. By the following year, my brother was staying out after midnight, stumbling home in a cloud of pot or sex. Under his mattress I found Polaroids of topless girls from school; in a shoebox, three hundred forty-two dollars. I saw the growing anger in his eyes, an emotion so comprehensive it affected most aspects of his life, even basketball. His joy in the game lessened, his shots were troubled by a larceny of spirit. He threw sucker punches at opposing players and no longer responded when reporters asked him for a quote. Toward the end of the season, his coach demoted him to second string, where he sat with the sophomores and the teammates who did not share his coordination or intense love for the game.

Even then, at my age, I understood what he wanted: he wanted someone to stand up to him, to stand in for our father. Within six months, he was arrested twice for shoplifting. He was suspended from school for keeping three dime bags of pot in his locker. My mother forced him into counseling; she accompanied him to juvenile court; when he was released, she grounded him for two months, a sentence that was shortened after he tore down his bedroom door, trying to escape from our house.

When he was beyond her control, beyond anyone's, she sent him to live with my uncle, who owned a farmhouse in Ohio. The rest is not difficult to understand. After two months he ran away. For a while he sent postcards, nondescript types that featured panoramic views of a city at night. He wrote mainly about the different jobs he held, as if he'd found some small satisfaction in them: he was almost always a busboy, and when he wasn't a busboy he worked at a community golf course, being both caddy and assistant greenskeeper. My mother asked him to come home many times, but he never did.

A year after he was sent to my uncle's, my mother and I sat on the front porch, commemorating that day and the sorrow it had brought us. We looked east, the direction the taxi had taken him to the airport. The back of my brother's head had been framed in the rear window, his long hair hanging in tight curls, himself too proud to look at us and betray his sadness. We sat there that night, the first anniversary of his departure, filled with longing and guilt. Sitting there, staring at the road, I was sure of two things in my life: my father had walked off this porch when I was three, never to return or send word of his location; eight years later he was followed by my brother. I felt the absence of these men in deep internal ways.

Sipping ginger ale and looking out at our street, my mother said, He was always your father's boy, as though this explained something essential about him.

I moved closer to her, our chairs almost touching. We stared down our street, rows of one-story houses, each marked with a single parkway tree. Gradually the sun became low and wide, until it finally dipped below the horizon, its color darkening to that of a plum. I sat there, almost touching my mother. Almost touching, she sat next to me. We both thought of my brother, and correspondingly, this made us think of my father, the ways we were connected to these men who had left us and what that would mean in our lives. We waited until it was dark, until the cool hand of evening touched our brows, and then silently—ever so silently—we went back inside.

Corporal

RICHARD BRAUTIGAN

Once I had visions of being a general. This was in Tacoma
during the early years of World War II when I was a child
going to grade school. They had a huge paper drive that was
brilliantly put together like a military career.

It was very exciting and went something like this: If
you brought in fifty pounds of paper you became a private
and seventy-five pounds of paper were worth a corporal's
stripes and a hundred pounds to be a sergeant, then spiraling pounds of paper leading upward until finally you arrived
at being a general.

I think it took a ton of paper to be a general or maybe
it was only a thousand pounds. I can't remember the exact
amount but in the beginning it seemed so simple to gather
enough paper to be a general.

I started out by gathering all the loose paper that was lying
innocently around the house. That added up to three or four
pounds. I'll have to admit that I was a little disappointed. I
don't know where I got the idea that the house was just filled
with paper. I actually thought there was paper all over the
place. It's an interesting surprise that paper can be deceptive.

I didn't let it throw me, though. I marshaled my energies
and went out and started going door to door asking people
if they had any newspapers or magazines lying around that
could be donated to the paper drive, so that we could win the
war and destroy evil forever.

An old woman listened patiently to my spiel and then she gave me a copy of *Life* magazine that she had just finished reading. She closed the door while I was still standing there staring dumbfoundedly at the magazine in my hands. The magazine was warm.

At the next house, nobody was home.

That's how it went for a week, door after door, house after house, black after block, until finally I got enough paper together to become a private.

I took my goddamn little private's stripe home in the absolute bottom of my pocket. There were already some paper officers, lieutenants and captains, on the block. I didn't even bother to have the stripe sewed on my coat. I just threw it in a drawer and covered it up with some socks.

I spent the next few days cynically looking for paper and lucked into a medium pile of *Collier's* from somebody's basement, which was enough to get my corporal's stripes that immediately joined my private's stripe under the socks.

The kids who wore the best clothes and had a lot of spending money and got to eat hot lunch every day were already generals. They had known where there were a lot of magazines and their parents had cars. They strutted military airs around the playground and on their way home from school.

Shortly after that, like the next day, I brought a halt to my glorious military career and entered into the disenchanted paper shadows of America where failure is a bounced check or a bad report card or a letter ending a love affair and all the words that hurt people when they read them.

The Quinceañera Text

ERIN FANNING

The present's wrapping paper crinkled in my hands. I shook it, but the box remained silent—not even a revealing thud. I wouldn't have heard it anyway, what with Juan, my baby brother, wailing from Tía Lupe's arms, and Papá singing along to Tío Jaime's mariachi band.

"Ana, hurry. Abuela's watching us." My cousin Consuela nodded at the present. "Could it be a cell phone?"

"It's the right size." I looked around. My grandmother winked at me from the other side of the patio. She wagged a finger then took a forkful of tamale, catching a scoop of shredded pork and popping it in her mouth just before it dropped to her lap.

Behind her, a table swelled with frijoles, tortillas, and pollo en mole. The smell of its chocolate sauce drifted across the patio. How many times had I helped Abuela chop the garlic, onions, and other ingredients that went into the dish? I knew her kitchen—the dried peppers hanging from the ceiling and Abuela's recipe book propped up against mixing bowls—better than my own bedroom

In the center of this food-mountain sat my Quinceañera cake. Red frosting flowers cascaded down one side of the four tiers, and a figurine of a woman with black hair and a white gown nestled on the top.

The color of the doll's hair and dress matched my own, but I didn't feel as elegant as she looked. And I certainly didn't feel like a woman. Even though that's what the celebration was all about, my "coming of age," as Papá said, my fifteenth birthday—La Quinceañera.

I longed to ditch the frilly dress, let down my hair, and throw on boots and jeans. I'd then saddle up my mare Esperanza and ride out into the desert surrounding our house. Instead, I was stuck as the center of attention.

"I'm sorry your Quinceañera had to be so, you know..." Consuela blushed and fiddled with a bow on her dress. "I didn't mean it's a bad party."

For a second, I felt a sliver of resentment, remembering Consuela's Quinceañera—the banquet hall, chandeliers, and gleaming dance floor. My anger, though, vanished when I saw the embarrassment on her face. "It's okay. If Papá hadn't lost his job then maybe it would have been different. But I really don't care."

The presents, of course, helped. And if one of those boxes contained a phone then my life would be complete. I'd no longer be one of the losers at school without a cell.

"You're too young," was Papá's reply when I asked for one.

Mamá, though, told me the real reason. "Too much money."

I picked up another box. "Consuela, watch for Mamá just a little while longer. She'll be pissed if she catches me going through these."

No reply.

I turned around. Consuela was texting away as usual.

"Oh, sorry," she said. "It's a mess—."

Mamá clapped her hands. "Time to open the gifts."

Everyone wandered over to us. Even Esperanza, ears pricked up, trotted to the corral fence. All eyes watched me as I opened present after present—turquoise earrings, midnight-blue cowboy boots, lip gloss—but no cell phone.

I tried to push away my disappointment, but it gripped me as tightly as Papá lassoing a calf. When the last present, a flat box without a card, was placed in my hands, I knew I wouldn't be getting what I wanted.

I yanked the paper off and opened the lid. Abuela's recipe book rested in a bed of tissue paper. "Recetas" was written across the cover in a spidery scrawl. I'd seen it about a million times, usually surrounded by pots and pans.

"Why?" My voice must have captured my confusion because Mamá frowned.

"Hija, a little gratitude," she hissed. Louder, she added, "A family tradition. The libro de recetas goes from grandmother to granddaughter on her Quinceañera."

Jaime and his band singing, "De Niña a Mujer," drowned her out. It was time for another tradition—a dance with Papá. He bowed and led me to a clear space on the patio. I caught a glimpse of Abuela, her shoulders slumped, shuffling to a chair.

Papá tripped on a patio stone and stumbled. "Lo siento," he said. "Your old Papá is a little stiff."

"I'm not exactly señorita suave."

It wasn't only my feet, though, that lacked smoothness. My heart felt brittle too. Papá twirled me around, and I glimpsed Abuela leaning back in her chair. She sank into the shadows, and her face disappeared into a streaky gray smudge, as if it were being erased. I pushed back a tear.

Other dancers joined us when the song ended. Mamá cursed me with her eyes, but Juan saved me when Lupe dumped him into Mamá's arms.

The libro de recetas sat where I'd left it on a loveseat. I flopped down and opened it to the first page. Smeared ink read, "1881, Guadalajara, Juanita Alvarez," my great-great grandmother. Flipping through the book, I stopped when I recognized Abuela's handwriting. I whispered some of the ingredients, "Canela, azúcar, caramelo." It sounded like poetry.

The setting sun flamed across the patio. Papá twirled Mamá, her arms encircling Juan, and Jaime serenaded Lupe. Consuela texted from the porch, unaware that Manuel, a friend from school, gave her a love-sick look.

"Te gusta?" Abuela said from behind me. Her dress billowed around her as she joined me on the loveseat. When had she lost so much weight? I scooted closer, remembering how her knees creaked when she kneeled at Mass that morning.

"I like it very much. Will you teach me some of Juanita's recipes?"

She smiled, her black eyes disappearing into the wrinkles lining her face. "I teach you everything I know."

I ran my fingers across the leather cover, tracing the word, "Recetas." It may not have been a cell phone, but it spoke to me all the same.

The Stoop

DONALD CAPONE

The bottom of the Italian ice is always the best, Samantha thought, as she flipped the chunk of ice over with the wooden tongue depressor to reveal the gooey underside. She sat on the stoop out front of her house, her favorite spot to watch the goings-on in the neighborhood. In her ten years she had seen everything—or so she thought. Her father once said that she was already jaded, that there was no hope for her now. The block had all the drama and comedy she could ever want; in fact, she preferred it to staying indoors and watching made-up crap on television. Anyway, the TV was broken again.

You want drama? Old man Kessler would come home drunk from work every Thursday night, stumble into the garbage cans out by the curb, then chase his lazy, good-for-nothing, long-haired, nineteen-year-old son from the house in a hail of curses and an occasional thrown shoe. The wailing Mrs. Kessler would try in vain to pull her husband back into the house. The son would take off in a huff, circle the block on foot, then come back and sit on his own stoop for hours while his father cooled off or passed out, whichever came first.

Comedy was covered, too. The spinster McMullen walked King, a hyperactive poodle, at precisely the same time every day: 8 a.m., 7 p.m., then again at 11 p.m. Which isn't so funny in and of itself. It was the matching outfits that she and the dog wore. It was the way she crouched down beside her doggie and encouraged him to deliver the goods. It was the way she used a plastic bag as a glove to lift the poop, then quickly turn the bag inside out. People thought she was nuts; Samantha's father just thought she needed a boyfriend.

But on this night, Samantha was the star. She was halfway done with the ice, just about ready to flip it again when she heard a muffled cry. The houses were all attached; it was summer and people had their windows open. Noises came at her from all directions. But this was different. It wasn't coming from someone's house. It sounded close— real close.

Samantha stopped scraping the ice and cocked her head to the side. When the sound came again, her eyes settled on the garbage can out front of her own house. She placed the Italian ice down on the stoop, and after a quick glance over her shoulder at her front door, walked to the curb. She held her hand over the lid of the can, her heart pounding as she tried to screw up the courage to lift the cover.

She wondered if anyone was watching now that she was the lead character in this little neighborhood play. Finally, with what she thought was a bit of dramatic flair, she grabbed the lid and snatched it off like she was performing a magic trick. A newborn baby was there, lying on a full trash bag. The baby's umbilical cord dangled off to one side. He moved his head and curled his little fists in protest, let out another cry.

He was the most fragile, beautiful thing Samantha had ever seen.

Samantha had never held a baby before, but how hard could it be? She reached in and touched him with both hands. The newborn slime caused her to quickly pull her hands away. She took off her sweatshirt, wrapped it around the baby, and gently lifted him from the garbage can. The baby stopped crying. She cradled him in her left arm, the way she'd seen women do sometimes. Samantha wondered if her own mother had ever done this to her, if she'd ever had the opportunity.

Samantha carefully climbed the front steps, then pushed open the door with her shoulder and backed into her apartment. Her father stood at the kitchen sink, washing the dishes from dinner.

"Dad?"

He turned around. "Oh, my god. Where did you—?"

"He was in the garbage can. Out front. Do you think his mother died?"

"Oh, Samantha, I hope not." Her father came over and pulled the sweatshirt back from the baby's face. "Looks like he was just born. His mother must still be out there."

"Can we keep him?"

Her father touched the baby's face, but didn't answer. He looked at Samantha, and his expression suggested that he was actually considering the notion. Then the doorbell rang and broke the spell. "Hello, sir. I'm Officer Jenkins. Mrs. Kessler across the street called us." The policeman came in and took the baby from Samantha. "We already found the mother."

"Is she okay?" Samantha asked.

"She's at the hospital. She'll be fine. She's a kid herself."

"Come on, Jenks," said a second officer, "let's get him to the ER."

Samantha and her father watched the policemen get in their car, turn on the lights, and speed off down the street. Samantha's father put his arm around her as they sat on the stoop. The Italian ice was still there, red liquid now. "Dad, why would Mom die? She was in the hospital and everything."

Her father was silent a moment. "I don't know, Sam. I don't know."

Soon the spinster McMullen emerged from her apartment, King following a pace behind. Their 7 p.m. walk. They each wore a blue shirt with a white stripe. Any moment now, old man Kessler would return home from work and start hassling his no-good nineteen-year-old son again.

The Last Stop

JENNY HALPER

The night before I turned thirteen we were speeding through Ohio, the radio pulsing with The Doors, the highway cutting a thin black knife through the flattest land I'd ever seen. I was sitting in the back seat, my forehead pressed against the window, waiting to spot swaying corn or, better yet, a scarecrow. Mostly there were just gas stations, appearing as exciting dots in the distance and rushing up on us with yellow lights and greasy men dragging long, uncombed beards. When I asked my father if we were going to stop, gesturing to the Jolly Rancher wrappers crinkling across the backseat, my mouth frozen with a cherry taste, my tongue permanently purple—the candies were all we'd eaten in days—he handed me a roll of bills and asked me to count them, and I did, thinking all the while of the city we had left and how, this time tomorrow, I would be thirteen and a grown-up and I would see the world with different eyes, the way you probably look at things differently after you've held a gun in your hands or watched a man killed. The way you look at people and think, I can make you disappear, although I would learn later that you can't really make anything disappear, not even the mother that you've never met, not even when you sit in the dark and close your eyes.

"I'm already at six," I said, meaning thousand, and the sun was at the point of setting when there weren't any colors, just a gray sky and a hint of a moon. My father took a sharp curve that made me fall sideways across the seat, pumping his foot on the gas, saying he loved Jim Morrison because the music made him feel like everything was about to start, like the fires hadn't been lit and the road was waiting for us to drive over it, all that blank space we needed to fill. When he talked like this he would cock his head to the left side of the car like he was hoping someone other than me would answer, like these were things a kid couldn't understand. I rested my elbows on the gray felt between the driver seat and the passenger seat, trying to swallow the music. "Sometimes," my father said wearily, "he just makes me want to have a cigarette."

Later that night, when the sky was as black as the road, my father pulled into a gas station with a Tiger Mart attached and told me to wait in the car. He was getting smokes, he said, but I knew he was also buying something for me, a surprise, or else he would have let me come inside with him. I wondered if he was buying a birthday cake. I wondered if he remembered tomorrow was my birthday. I crawled into the driver's seat, put my hands on the steering wheel, and turned the wheel to the right and the left, thinking of all the places I could go if I was old enough, if I could see above the dashboard, if I could tell the gas from the brake, if I could choose songs of my own to push me from one life to the next.

Forsythia

JACQUELINE KOLOSOV

Miranda pulls the old Chevy into the drive. A neat row of daffodils and grape iris border the front walk. Here, too, forsythia blooms, the spiraling branches like captured sunshine. Beyond, the house is white-washed brick.

When Grace Wickersham steps onto the porch, Miranda's hands instinctively curve around her swelling belly. "Please come in." Grace's voice is husky, nervous.

This is only the second time they've met.

Inside, Miranda takes in the room in one long sweep. In the corner, there is an overstuffed sofa covered with red poppies. On the sofa a big, gray dog lies drowsing.

Grace's husband, Matt, enters with a plate of cookies and three glasses of juice. Miranda smiles at the bright drink chock full of vitamins. Surely she is the reason why they're drinking orange juice at three o'clock in the afternoon.

Crumbs fall into their laps as they circle around the subject that has brought them together. How could she possibly tell them that at night she lies awake thinking about keeping him, for she's sure he is a boy? In bed, with the curtains drawn back, the sky becomes a magician's cape, and the edges of reality are softened.

Morning restores the sharp outlines. In the kitchen, her mother's face is a grid of gray planes, and she is wearing the catsup-stained factory uniform that always smells of sweat and tomatoes.

"We have two extra bedrooms upstairs," Grace Wickersham says, her eyes meeting Miranda's. "The one beside ours will be the baby's room. The other is for guests."

"What Grace is trying to say is we'd like you to be our guest for the remainder of the pregnancy," Matt adds. "We'd like to help you in any way we can."

Miranda is reminded of the neat rows of daffodils, the forsythia, their delicate branches swaying in the breeze. "Thank you," she says, "but I live at home with my mother and my sister Kate."

"We didn't mean to imply—" Matt says, fiddling with the ice in his glass.

"Do you think I could see the baby's room?" Miranda asks.

"I'll wait down here," Matt says, as the two women move toward the staircase.

Grace opens the door.

It is everything a child's room should be. The walls are a warm, honey gold. There is a border of crayon-bright sunflowers and frogs running along the floor. A refinished crib sits beside the window; beside it, a rocker.

"I spent the past month getting the room ready," Grace says.

Miranda nods, unable to imagine how it would feel to be an expectant mother painting flowers and animals on the walls of a room in her own home, then sitting down in the rocker to admire her handiwork, a cup of tea warming her hands.

"Would you like to see the extra room?" Grace asks her then.

"All right."

Down the hallway, Grace opens another neatly painted door, and Miranda beholds a double bed, heaped with pillows. A single dresser holds a crystal vase filled with forsythia. White lace curtains adorn the windows. The room is exactly what Miranda would have chosen for herself.

"We thought it would be nice to get to know each other better," Grace tells her.

Miranda watches the play of sunlight in Grace's long auburn hair. She would like to take the silver-backed brush from the dresser and run it through Grace's hair. She would like to tell Grace that the baby's father is on a scholarship at the University of Michigan. He, too, comes from one of the factory towns, but he managed to get out. Miranda doesn't even know when she will see him again.

What she does know is she cannot move into this sunny room. If she were to enter into the inner spaces of this life, how would she ever find the strength to say goodbye?

On the drive back to Ipswich, Miranda listens to Bruce Springsteen sing about love and amusement parks. The song brings back the summer her father took her and her sister to a carnival. Miranda's front tooth was loose, and as they walked through the fairgrounds, she kept wiggling it with her tongue. She wanted to loosen it, but she didn't want it to fall out there. Miranda was afraid of losing that tooth, afraid of missing out on the tooth fairy's visit.

Miranda's father held her hand and Kate's. They passed the Ferris wheel with its Lifesaver-colored lights, the shooting gallery with its toys. Even with her small hand in his, Miranda hadn't felt secure.

Her father, a very tall man with rough, reddish whiskers, looked down. "What's the matter, little mouse?" he asked. "Aren't you having fun? You're supposed to be having fun."

After that, Miranda tried hard to have fun. She wanted to please her father. She wanted to show him that she was a good girl.

That next summer when the carnival returned, Miranda

had already lost half a dozen more teeth. And that next summer, her father was already gone.

When Miranda told her mother that she was going to have a baby, her mother stayed silent for a long time, her hopes and fears interlaced as tightly as her hands. "I just don't want you to wind up like me," her mother said finally. "I want you to have more choices in your life."

Miranda understood what her mother was saying. Don't become a woman with a high school diploma, a job at the catsup factory, a mortgage on a ramshackle house, two daughters, and no husband.

And yet, Miranda thinks, *you did your best.*

Miranda nears the Ipswich exit and recalls the daffodils and the forsythia, the hopping frogs and sunflowers, the white wicker rocker, and understands—deep within herself, where her baby stirs—that, by giving up her child to them, she won't be doing her best for him, but she will be doing the best she can.

And this, she knows, *this* will have to be enough.

Fifteen Fathers

ALAN STEWART CARL

At noon, Dad begins to flip from game to game to game. He has fifteen fantasy football teams and needs to follow all these players. A pile of quarterbacks. Running backs. Receivers and all that, too. He's made me memorize their names and jersey numbers so I know when to cheer. But twenty minutes in, I do it wrong again. I say: "Boldin caught the ball!" And Dad slaps the side of his chair and says: "We don't need Boldin to catch the ball. Get your head in the game."

An hour later, Mom wanders through the living room and drops the classifieds on the ottoman. Dad rolls them into a tube and sticks them at her stomach. "My day," he says, tilting his head to see around her. "It's always your day," she says and I think she's going to say more, but as soon as Dad looks at her, she takes a step back. "You don't think I deserve this?" Dad says, leaning forward. "Can't I win something for once?" And I think how strange that is. He always wins. And always loses. "I've seen his teams," I say to Mom, but she looks at me like maybe I'm not feeling well. Then she takes the paper from Dad and leaves the room.

But it's true. I've seen all of Dad's teams. Every one of them is named The Big Dogs, but some are winners and some are losers. 7-3 and 3-7 and 10-0 and 1-9 and everything else. It's like he's all these different people in all these different places. Which could be cool. To be in different places. Like maybe there's a me who's tall and dating Eva Ruiz. And another me who's got ten brothers. And maybe there's a me who never came home the other week, who just kept running and running and now he lives all alone in the woods, under the trees. And what if I could be that me right now? What if I could pick and choose who to be and who to never be? What if that's what Dad wants, too? What if he just hasn't figured out how to do it right?

By the time the three o'clock games begin, I know how to help him. I say I have to go to the bathroom but I head outside instead. I find Mom's garden shears and her gloves. I stand on the back patio, stretching out to where the satellite cable runs down the siding. I expect sparks. Fire. But when I cut the cord, the bottom part just falls away. For a moment, I watch the cable swing, then I hear Dad's voice coming from inside. He's shouting: "Goddamn satellite. Where's the goddamn phone?" Through the window, I can see him hurrying around, frantic until he finds the phone. He shouts into the receiver and then he listens.

I imagine the operator is saying there's no problem. All the games are going exactly as he wants, everyone is winning. And I imagine Dad is hearing this in all his different places—all those places sliding together, the 7-3s and 1-9s and 6-4s becoming hundreds. More than enough. I imagine him hanging up. Smiling. And the thought of this makes me smile, too.

That's when Dad sees me in the window. He lowers the phone. And I know what the operator has really been saying. She's told him the problem is on his end. I want to shout "It's on all the ends." And I know one of my dads would understand what I mean. I know one of my dads would laugh and walk away. But that's not the dad who sees me. That's not the dad whose face goes red at the sight of the cable dangling free.

The Bracelet

ANN ANGEL

Trevor never said hello when he came into my house. He just made himself comfortable on one of the kitchen stools. Today was no different, only when I sat beside him, he pressed warm metal into my palm and closed my hand around it.

"Here," he said. Trevor was a guy of few words.

I opened my palm to reveal a silver charm bracelet. A series of interlocked silver loops were held together with heart-shaped beads of burnished silver. A small loop linked a silver heart locket to the center. The bracelet was beautiful.

"Happy birthday," Trevor said. I looked from the bracelet to him, gauging what it might signify. "It's your birthday, right?"

"Yeah, it's my birthday." I closed my hand around the bracelet, feeling its weight.

Trevor combed his fingers through curls that never looked combed.

The bracelet seemed like something you'd give a girl you thought you loved. I wracked my brain, trying to recall anything that would indicate we were heading in that direction.

Trevor and I had only been on two dates so far. His eyes searched my face to read my reaction.

"Thank you," I said, unsure what to think. I slid my thumbnail under the heart locket and popped it open. Someone had inserted a slip of shocking pink paper in each half of the heart. One side said, "Worth Loving." The other was simply "XOXO." The handwriting looked girlish, nothing like the cramped style I'd glimpsed on Trevor's last Shakespeare test, writing out Hamlet's curse. I looked again to see if my best friend Kat had written these, but they were too artsy for Kat's round handwriting.

I imagined a sales clerk standing over a jewelry display whiling away time until closing. She would chew on a pen, trying to decide what fairy godmother wish to print before carefully tucking notes into each locket. Was it simply luck that I was holding a note declaring me "Worth Loving"?

Trevor cleared his throat and said, "I asked which is it."

"Which what?" The bracelet must have cost plenty.

"Birthday."

"Oh, sixteen. My family doesn't do parties," I explained before he could ask. "My mom usually makes a dinner for our birthdays. I think Kat's invited to dinner though." My voice trailed off. He would already know Kat was coming. They shared about four classes and talked a lot. In fact, I had always thought those two would make a good couple and was surprised when Trevor asked me out.

"So," Trevor said, "sweet sixteen and you can't say you've never been kissed?"

"I've been kissed plenty." Of course Trevor would know that. We spent part of our last date making out on his parents' couch in front of the TV.

I looked at the bracelet to cover the blush that warmed my face. Had Trevor searched through lockets to make sure his said "Worth Loving"? If he'd gone to the trouble of asking someone with neat handwriting to print this message for me, it meant something.

I wasn't sure how I felt about him though.

"This bracelet is really pretty," I said. But I couldn't accept it. I didn't like Trevor enough to call him "Worth Loving."

"Yeah, I thought so." He spoke so offhandedly I was surprised. "I gotta show up for track practice or coach will kill me." He was off the stool, brushing a kiss on my cheek as he passed, and almost to the back door before he turned and added, "Maybe I'll come over later. After dinner."

He was gone before I had a chance to respond.

I let silver links slide between my fingers into the palm of my hand.

My mother came in with the twins arguing behind her. She set groceries down on the counter and turned to Will and Josh. "Boys! I told you to knock it off in the grocery store. And in the bakery. Now I'm telling you to knock it off in this house, before I lose my ever-loving mind!"

Josh punched Will in the shoulder. "Yeah, jackass."

"Josh and Will! Get Kelly's birthday cake out of the van!"

I warned, "That cake will be in pieces if you let one of them get it." I stood and put the bracelet on the counter. "I'll get it."

"What's that?" Mom asked.

"A gift from Trevor."

She picked it up. "Are you and Trevor serious?"

"I didn't think so. But he's coming over later."

I could see my mom mentally counting plates, so I assured her, "He knows he's not invited for dinner."

"When Aunt Joanie received diamond earrings from her fireman, it meant they were serious," Mom said.

"I hear you." I took the bracelet and headed upstairs. I said, "This isn't the same."

But I wondered just what the value of this bracelet was to Trevor. A kiss? More?

When Kat showed up later, she played with my jars and tubes of unused make-up.

As she lined her eyes, Kat told me she was with Trevor when he "jacked" the bracelet. "The notes were inside. They don't mean anything." Strokes of black arched across each eyelid, making cat wings. "I told Trevor I needed a present. Those bracelets were close to the door when we walked out of Hot Destiny."

My stomach turned sour. "So, the bracelet is stolen?" I stared at the silver loops and hearts. "Such a loaded gift to mean nothing."

I dropped the bracelet on the dresser.

Kat eyed it.

"Do you want the bracelet?"

"Of course not. He gave it to you."

"I don't really like it," I said.

Come to think of it, I didn't really like Kat all that much right now. And I didn't think I could stand Trevor. I told her, "Go ahead. Take the bracelet. It's yours."

You Cannot Make Me

MILES GARETT WATSON

Coconut, green olives, apricots—the foods I wouldn't touch the day Ms. Staggs supervised a taste test in our second-grade classroom. I kissed Susan on the lips—we were going to get married—but her father took a job in Akron before Halloween. Candy corn, those caramel apples from Mrs. Talley. At Christmas, I exchanged gold necklaces with Jill, a shimmering *J* dangling from hers. We did not kiss. I peed my pants the day Ms. Staggs made me wait during a spelling test. Spell *beauty*, spell *accident*, spell *shame*. The ice storm in January, the Sunday morning at Valley Baptist I accepted Jesus, not fully understanding what that meant. Yellow squash, lima beans, asparagus—the foods my father demanded I try at Sunday lunches. You cannot make me, I said. I sat for eternities to prove it, sat on my hands long past bedtime. Spell *stubborn*. Who was more, my father or me? He taught me how to hit a curveball, though I wasn't yet in Little League. I was in Buddy League, and my father coached the team. We hit off a pitching machine, its pitches always straight as a ray of sunshine. And always the same speed. I was left-handed. I could pole a ball down the line, cruise around the bases—twice if I really wanted. I played first base. I could move left as easily as right, dig a ball out of the dirt. Halfway through summer, our catcher fell off his roof, and my father asked me to switch positions. A left-handed catcher's mitt impossible to find—use your first base mitt, he said. The shin guards hung loose from my knees, the orange chest protector thunked every time a pitch slid off the edge of my glove. I could taste the breath each ball knocked from my lungs. I could taste red clay, the dust that chalked my uniform, the foul balls that rattled my mask. I don't want to do this, I said. Spell *team*, my father said, spell *sacrifice*.

Jew School

SONIA PILCER

"I don't know what you do, who you're with," my mother said as we rode the bus to Yeshiva Rabbi Soleveichik on 185th Street, where my father insisted she enroll me. "It's better here. You'll be with Jewish children, not the goyim on the street."

I despised Judaism. Lighting candles to remember the dead. Holidays and high holidays, which introduced yet more taboos. Why did they talk about *shvartzes* like sub-humans? As if Jews were a different race and we mustn't consort with anyone else.

My mother's inconsistent rites of observation! Bacon and ham were okay, but no pork chops. Spare ribs from the Chinese restaurant were okay, too. The two-faced double standards for inside and outside the house. Every Saturday, my mother turned on the radio to listen to the *Make-Believe Ballroom,* watched the *Million Dollar Movie,* and so did I. But if I was going outside, I had to observe Shabbos and not wear pants.

"You must look decent. They tried to destroy us," she told me. "Now we must show how well we dress."

For my interview with the rabbi, my teased hairdo was forcibly reduced by fifty percent. My mother made me wear a blue pleated skirt with a white cotton blouse—Israel's colors, she reminded me. But I sported my black leather roach-killer boots. I was a slum goddess, after all.

Inside the red brick building, all the boys wore yarmulkes. As they raced through the halls, their arms filled with books, the strings of their *tzitzit* streamed behind them like leashes. The girls walked quietly. Upon noticing me, they began to whisper among themselves. One boy grunted loudly, "Ugh." As I seemed to scratch my head, I gave them all a subtle third finger.

In the elevator, my mother raised her slip. She then pulled down the hem of her blue wool dress. "All right?" she asked, turning around. "I copied this pattern from *Vogue.*"

We entered a musty-smelling office, papers strewn over the old, scratched-up desk and on the chair, and leather-bound volumes from ceiling to floor. As the rabbi looked up from the text on his desk, I could see his long, white beard, white *peyes,* and sharp blue eyes.

He opened a book with large Hebrew letters. "Will you read these?" he said, pointing with his finger.

"I don't know how," I said, staring down blankly, but of course recognizing the *aleph, bet, daled, gimel, hay . . .*

"Haven't your parents sent you to Hebrew school?"

I nodded. Our text, *The History of the Jewish People,* started with Abraham and Moses, through Disraeli, to Ben Gurion, Leonard Bernstein, and Bernie Schwartz, known to his fans as Tony Curtis.

The teacher was a balding, dogmatic man who despised questions, especially from girls. A crocheted yarmulke with a black circle in its center was bobby-pinned to his short hair. When he turned around to write on the blackboard, I imagined shooting a rubber band and paper clip. Bull's-eye!

"Young lady," the rabbi demanded, "don't make me angry. What's the first letter of the Hebrew alphabet?"

"Aleph." I nearly spat the word.

His blue eyes observed me from their pink pockets. "You don't want to go to yeshiva? Why? Don't you want an education?"

Yeshiva meant four hours of religion in addition to regular school. I crossed my arms. "I'm an atheist," I said, having come across the word in *The Fountainhead* by Ayn Rand.

"Don't be rude," my mother misunderstood. "She doesn't mean that," she apologized, cuffing me on the back of my neck.

The rabbi studied me, shaking his head. "You speak because you don't know. Is that what you want? To be stupid like the rest of the world?"

"I don't want to go to yeshiva," I declared, wondering why Jews always thought they were so smart.

"Do you think you'd be happier going to public school?" he asked.

I nodded.

"You know there won't be many white children," he said.

"I don't care," I said.

"You like the colored?" my mother asked. "When they beat you up, you weren't so happy."

In sixth grade, a group of older girls followed me after school. "Balloonhead!" they called. "Shake it, don't break it, took your momma nine months to make it." Their taunts grew louder. "She thinks she's hot." I walked fast, knowing Broadway wasn't far. They followed on my heels. "Hey girl," someone called, "when I talk to you, you listen." I started to run. Suddenly, a girl grabbed my arms from behind and threw me down. I landed on my knees, the concrete ripping my stockings. My knees bled as I made my way home. My mother had found my bloody stockings in the garbage.

"Have you no shame?" the rabbi demanded suddenly.

I stared at the ground, not to meet his stinging blue eyes.

"After what your parents went through," he said.

I crossed my arms, not answering him.

"Say something!" my mother urged. "What's wrong with you?"

I shifted my weight to the other foot.

"We can't force you to learn." The rabbi shrugged. "She doesn't belong here, Mrs. Palovsky."

My mother nodded. "I didn't think so. It was my husband's idea. In Poland, his family was very religious."

The rabbi was through with us, but my mother continued. "My family was assimilated. Still they took us away and murdered everyone."

"We must honor the memory of those who perished," the rabbi said, standing up slowly. His dark jacket was stained. "May everything work out for the best, God willing."

"Are you happy now?" she asked as we walked out of the building. "Now you can rot on the street with your juvenile delinquent friends."

"They're not juvenile delinquents," I insisted. "They just like to dress tough."

"But, Zosha, you belong with these people? Their families drink and the husbands beat up the wives. *Paskudnik!* Why can't you be normal — like Daddy and me?"

Disorder

SAMANTHA DAVIS

"You know," Dr. Wartegan began, flipping through Lisa's file, "when I was an adolescent, there were few treatments available. Teenagers were left to suffer through these years without any help. And it was awful for the parents."

Lisa nodded, her eyes flitting around the doctor's office, the white walls adorned with framed recognition, the desk with its neat piles of labeled folders. Dr. Wartegan's laptop screensaver displayed generic tropical scenes. She watched as a close-up of a hammock between two palm trees dissolved into a wide-angle shot of a white-sand beach and an impossibly turquoise sea.

"I had one friend who suffered for years," the doctor continued, jotting notes onto her prescription pad as she spoke. "An acquaintance really... she had such severe attention problems. They were just starting to medicate back then; it really hadn't caught on yet. Terrible grades, academic probation, you name it. She was so disorganized, you wouldn't believe her dorm room. She never did her homework... I'd come into her room and find her sitting on her windowsill writing poems instead." The doctor looked up at Lisa and smiled, a theatrically sad smile. Lisa tried to smile back, but it caught; her face wouldn't cooperate and it came out as more of a grimace.

Concern fell across Dr. Wartegan's face like a sheet falling across a stage, a set change. The doctor reached out and patted

Lisa's hand. Lisa found herself stiffening, trying not to recoil from those cold fingers with their French-manicured nails.

"She suffered from bouts of depression too," the doctor continued, returning her attention to Lisa's file. "And so of course, she self-medicated..." The doctor looked back at Lisa and raised her eyebrows pointedly. "Drug and alcohol abuse were far more common back then."

Lisa looked down at her feet. The tattered hem of her jeans brushed the floor. Her black ballet flats had nearly broken through at the toes, the leather worn to a thin gray. Her mother had tried to convince Lisa to lose those shoes, not to mention the nearly translucent T-shirt she'd been holding onto since eighth grade. But she'd gotten the T-shirt with Jake, at the Screaming Phobics concert, and the shoes were comfortable, reassuring somehow. She'd refused her mother on both counts.

"Did she... your friend... have a boyfriend?" Lisa bit her lip after speaking, unsure how or why the question had slipped out. Sometimes the words still misbehaved, popping out like that, acting on their own volition. Dr. Wartegan looked up abruptly, her features hard with alarm, though they quickly softened.

"She didn't really..." the doctor began, and her eyes grew distant, focused on some spot just to Lisa's left. "She always wanted one, was always falling for different guys, each of them out of her reach. She'd listen to music and believe all of that mythology of romantic love... but I don't remember her ever having a boyfriend." The doctor shook her head and turned back to the prescription pad. "She was more of an acquaintance, really."

Lisa watched as the doctor carefully tore three sheets from the prescription pad.

"Kids really had to struggle back then," the doctor said, handing the papers to Lisa. "We just hadn't the pharmacological understanding; we didn't know the treatment possibilities yet." The doctor stood, smoothing her pressed white coat. Lisa followed her lead, standing as well.

"What about you? How have you been feeling, Lisa?"

Lisa swallowed. "Okay. Fine."

"And your grades?"

"They're pretty good."

"That's good. And things with your mother? Better?"

"Yes. Better." Lisa hesitated, dropping her head and looking again at her scuffed shoes. "We haven't been fighting much at all." She eyed the file on Wartegan's desk, wondering what her mother had written on this week's report.

"Good. That's good." The doctor opened the office door. "You need to tell me if problems come up. You know we can adjust your dosage of Prysothene."

"I know," Lisa said. Raising her eyes to meet Dr. Wartegan's gaze, she repeated the doctor's oft-repeated mantra. *"There's no need to suffer."*

The doctor smiled, holding the office door open and stepping aside to allow her patient to leave. Lisa exited as directed, but turned before the doctor could retreat. "Your... acquaintance," Lisa said, feeling her cheeks flush as the doctor knit her brow. Her throat tightened, resisting, but Lisa pressed out her question. "What happened to her? I mean... later? When she grew up."

Dr. Wartegan stiffened, almost imperceptibly. "Honestly, I don't know. She went west to college, and everyone lost touch with her."

Lisa shrugged. "She disappeared. You lost touch. I guess that happens sometimes."

The doctor nodded, her eyes fixed again on some distant spot beyond her patient's face. "I guess that's right. She disappeared." Her eyes cleared and she returned her gaze to meet that of her sixteen-year-old patient, taking in the limp, dark hair; the wide, green eyes; the faded T-shirt with its odd jumble of symbols. "But you don't have to suffer like that. You'll never have to suffer like that."

"Thank you, Dr. Wartegan."

Lisa left the office, making her way out through the waiting room of teenagers, some accompanied by their tense, pale-faced parents. She descended twelve floors in the empty elevator and exited onto the street. The sun forced her to squint, but she could still make out a trash bin at the end of the block. She started walking towards it, then broke into a run. Upon reaching the barrel, she shredded the papers from Dr. Wartegan's prescription pad and released them into the trash, the tiny shreds of paper falling like snow. A few pieces caught in a breeze and escaped into the street or drifted down the sidewalk like sauntering pedestrians. The rest landed amidst discarded sandwich halves, crumpled newspapers, empty aluminum cans, and cigarette butts. Lisa exhaled, smiling slightly, then turned and walked back into the sun.

The Perpetual Now

DANIEL LEVIN BECKER

Sitting in the school auditorium and waiting for a small pianist to massage her way through a Fauré piece that writhed and writhed but just would not die, Henry remembered what his sister had once told him: that he must never wish to be done with something, no matter what it was, for that was tantamount to wishing seconds, minutes, hours, days of his life away. The piece ended moments later. He applauded like everyone else, but did not know how to feel.

The next morning he decided to live in the perpetual now. That day he invested himself fully in every moment, ready to be caught unawares by the next. In the shower, he thought about the beauty of domesticated water. At breakfast, he chewed slowly. In geometry, he ignored the lesson as usual, but spent the period very intently trying to estimate, to within a hundred, how many hairs were left on Mr. Radzinski's head. By sundown, he could not wait to go to sleep, but, wary of wishing the evening away, stayed up yawning until his usual bedtime.

In bed at last, it seemed to him that he was lying not horizontally but at an angle of between ten and thirty-five degrees.

The next morning, it occurred to him that sleep might be irreconcilable with the perpetual now. He wasn't going to stop sleeping, of course—but couldn't he do something productive with the time he was?

That night, he began taking notes in order to critique the accuracy and clarity of his dreams. *But who were those people and what were they doing painting your sister's room?* he would scrawl, barely awake, on the nearest available surface. Or: *Why would you photocopy the bark of a tree? Also, how?* He told his parents when they asked about the notes covering the table and walls around his bed, as well as his left hand and forearm, that he was doing it to eliminate the fanciful and unlikely and useless from his dreaming state, and eventually from his waking state, too. *It is physically impossible to do that in a canoe.* His parents smiled at him and looked at one another, as if to say it's just a phase and let's hope it ends soon.

It did not end for some months, and then one day Henry woke up terribly, oppressively bored. From then on, he left his dreams alone.

Bullhead

LEIGH ALLISON WILSON

Every story is true and a lie. My mother tells a story about the love of her life. It's a simple one, but she always cries when she tells it and looks right through me, as though I hadn't been born. Something about the detail makes me feel there's a sadness in the world that will last until the rushing crack of doom.

It goes like this: In the forties, when she was a teenaged girl in Tennessee, my mother fell in love with the boy next door. That same year, the government decided to build dams all over the state. As if some crazy rainstorm had come and gone, pristine new lakes puddled the landscape from Knoxville to Memphis. One lake formed right over my mother's hometown—people lost their homes, their businesses, their graveyards, their farmland and, in some cases, their hearts. On the night before the government moved everybody out of her hometown, my mother and the love of her life, this boy next door, made love in my mother's bedroom. Her parents were at a prayer meeting, praying for dry land, I guess, like Noah. This boy was sweet, was kind, was smart and generous and lovely to look at; this boy was the love of her life. He moved with his family to Texas the next day and she never saw him again.

Except: Once a year she rents a rowboat and goes out on the lake that has drowned her old hometown. She drops a penny over the side, right over the place where her old house must be. Fifty years, fifty pennies. She imagines them drifting downward, all those pennies, drifting through the murky lake water, startling the catfish and bullhead, each penny listing into the open window of her bedroom and falling at last onto the pillow where she once lay with her head against the love of her life, the boy next door. She imagines their ghost love showered by pennies; she imagines this love beyond all loves glittering with gold. Then she rows back to shore and back to my father and me and the life that can't compete with memory.

Every story is true and a lie. The true part of this one is: Love and the memory of love can't be drowned. The lie part is that this is a good thing.

The Call

JON ANDERSEN

"Jimmy... honey."

It was like an electric shock, that weird caught-between-worlds pulse that goes through you when you've screwed up replacing an outlet and got yourself between a black wire and a white wire. Then a full body smack: I was up kneeling on my bed in the pitch black, taut and ready.

I listened.

Just me quick-breathing and my blood chugging in my head. My eyes strained for light and my ears strained to hear my mother's voice again, or maybe her step on the stairs. There was the sound of my fan on low, turning and clicking, turning and clicking. Over maybe like the next five minutes I just really slowly uncoiled, listening, and looking the whole time. The window was open, but there wasn't even a breeze. An occasional bug knocked itself against the screen, then back into the night. The neighbors' house was dark and quiet and looked plunked down there under the stars. Their kids' bikes and toys were scattered around the driveway. They looked like echoes, I thought. Can something look like an echo?

Eventually, I was lying there again, but I didn't go back to sleep. I rolled and sat on the edge of the bed, pushed myself up. When I stood my legs were shaky. I walked toward the hall. I didn't want to wake Sis or Dad or the baby, and I just tried to creak along as softly as I could, avoiding the noisiest boards. Sis's room was next to mine on the right. I stopped there for a couple minutes outside her closed door. Nothing. I knew that she was sleeping in her single bed with the baby on her chest. They were in love like nothing I knew. At the end of the hall, I stopped at the top of the stairwell and could see Dad's foot at the end of the couch down in the den, in blue, flickering light. He was in his usual spot—asleep in front of the TV with the sound off.

I knew it then and I'll say it now: it wasn't a dream. It wasn't the fan, it wasn't the woman or the kids next door, it wasn't Sis talking in her sleep or the baby crying out, and it sure as hell wasn't my father. My mother had called to me. Gently. But now that she had my attention, she didn't have anything else to say, and I haven't heard her since.

Between Practice and Perfection

AZIZAT DANMOLE

At thirteen, the other girls in your gymnastics class are strong and graceful while you are not. You even used to take ballet, but no one would believe it, looking at you. The way you flop around, awkwardly moving your hands and feet as you attempt each exercise. The older girls are on the uneven bars, and they swing from one bar to the other and then back again. Their long bodies are extended, their toes pointed, and their hands never miss the bar, even when they back-flip in between. The younger girls in your class are not as graceful, but fast and energetic. They tumble and twist. They do forward and backward rolls and stay in line. You cannot do a cartwheel. You cannot do a pull up and you cannot roll forward or backward without going sideways.

Ashley Anders, the best girl in your class, is an ex-ballet dancer, five feet even, an inch shorter than you, and so light on her feet that she sails from one move to the next. If there were a way to do an entire floor exercise routine where only one foot touched the mat the entire time, she would be the first to figure it out. You watch her hanging out with the girls from the Intermediate team as they eat yogurt and graham crackers and watch the girls from the Elite team, picking out who has the best landings and routines and chance for going pro. Ashley Anders is nice to everyone, and occasionally she has tried to help you, but to no avail.

Ashley Anders has rung the "success gong," a desk gong that is sounded when a gymnast achieves a goal, three times in the past week for being the first in her class to land a vault combination, a successful landing after dismounting from her bar routine, and for getting to perform at talent night with the Elite girls. The smallest girl on your team rang the gong for landing her round-off. Another girl on your team rang the gong for her handstand on the uneven bars, which she did only one week after recovering from a broken foot. You rang the gong when you learned to stand on the beam without falling off.

When it is time to start practicing aerial cartwheels, you pull Ashley Anders aside and ask her to explain it to you. Maybe watching movements is not the way you learn. Maybe you learn differently.

"How do you do this?" you ask.

"Like this," she says, putting her hand behind her back and cartwheeling like she had springs on the balls of her feet.

"Just put a hand behind your back," she says.

You try, but your hand touches the mat during your half-cartwheel.

She offers to help and supports your waist while you put a hand behind your back and try again, but your one hand is not used to supporting all your weight, and you go right over, kicking her in the nose in the process. When you right yourself, you apologize profusely, but Ashley is holding her nose and frowning. She walks wordlessly away from you, and the two of you avoid each other, and you are back to being on your own.

School is a welcome break from the gym. In art class you are asked to choose a picture to copy for your first assignment, and you choose a picture of Ashley Anders that you stole from the *Rising Stars* bulletin board at the gym. Although the picture is hard to copy, you learn that with a brushstroke or pencil mark you can give the picture an appearance of flying or flipping or twisting—the kind of grace that you only have in your dreams. When you have finished the body with only the face left to copy, you copy your face instead of Ashley's. You look graceful and perfect.

You go home and practice in the backyard, using the soft, thick grass as a mat and an old, long block of wood as a balance beam. When you go back to the gym, you still cannot do a forward roll or a cartwheel. When you try a floor exercise, you sprain your ankle. When you try the vault, you break your nose.

Your mother assures you that you are at an awkward age, and she buys you a new leotard and purchases a "Gymnast on Board" sign at the gym's gift counter. She sticks it in the rear window of the mini-van that she takes you to practice in. You assure yourself that with practice you will get better. You buy mats and wrist guards, thinking that with the right equipment, anything is possible.

During every class, you strain muscles or fall awkwardly off equipment, and when you overhear the Elite girls laughing, you think they are making fun of you. When you come home, you work out your frustration in your sketches, which even you have noticed are improving. A few months later, when the Elite girls are getting ready for their competition, you are getting ready to enter your paintings into the school's annual art fair contest. When Ashley Anders wins a medal for floor exercise, you win three out of five categories in the art fair for your *Dreams* collection, where your pictures of Ashley Anders are included among pictures that you have sketched of children in the park, your father at work on the garage, and your own self-portrait.

Your teachers tell you that the way you capture actions in a series of strokes is beautiful, and at the end of the night, when you see your self-portrait in the dim light of the display case, you don't look so awkward anymore.

How to Raise a Happy Dog

ERIKA RECORDON

The dog is old, and arthritic, so it's difficult for him to walk from one side of the lawn to the other. A year ago, Sasha could still inspire him to get up and eat the heads off her mother's daffodils, but these days he shows no interest.

When she looks at him now, Sasha says to herself, he is still my happy dog. This is what the vet told her, two weeks ago, when they brought the dog in for a checkup. They drove to the office together—Sasha, her mother, and her father—because they were all afraid of what they might be told. *He may tell us we need to do something*, her mother said. And though she did not say what the thing was, they all knew.

On the drive to the vet's office, Sasha felt anxious and thought of the things the family could have done better for the dog. We could have pet him more often, and fed him organic food, she thought. We could have let him sleep inside the house instead of out in the garage on a worn-out pillow.

The waiting room was white. There was only one couch, small and also white, so the three of them had to sit close together on it. They did not talk about the dog, who they knew was being examined in some other white room nearby. Instead, her mother talked about their neighbors who were robbed, but not harmed, and her father talked about the return of the 1918 influenza. *When it comes back*, he said.

Our government will not protect us. His eyes were stuck on his daughter. He said, *There is no federally mandated plan of action. You need a certain kind of mask, and there aren't enough to go around.*

Sasha sat very still and tried to make herself invisible. This was something she was learning how to do. She closed her eyes and thought about wind pushing through trees. She thought about her red dog running through an all white heaven.

The vet came out wearing a white coat and a head of clean smelling hair. He had a gentle voice, and a bright, hygienic smile. The smell around him was wonderful. Sasha was beginning to notice men. This is a good man, she thought. He helps sick animals feel better. What she liked best was the way he clicked his pen between sentences. It was such a cheerful sound. *Your dog is still happy,* the vet said. Click. *The pain could be much worse.* Click. Click. *Keep up the anti-inflammatories.* Click. What Sasha wanted just then was to leap up and kiss the vet on the mouth. But her mother's hand was there, pressing down on her shoulders.

Then the dog came out and met the family with his patient, friendly eyes. They all crowded around him, excited by the good news, and rubbed his back vigorously. *Here is our dog,* they said. *Here is our good dog!*

On the drive home, no one spoke. They were each listening to the world with a special kind of attention now, and besides there was nothing left to say. Everything was fine. Sasha listened. There was the radio announcer talking about an inbound traffic jam. There was the dog's breath, and there was the distant sound of music. Someone on their street was learning to play the piano.

This is a happy dog, Sasha thought as they turned into the driveway. And she thought it again when she watched her father lift the dog from the car and set him back onto the ground. His legs were weak and unnaturally bowed. His back was an empty bowl. *This is my happy dog,* she said aloud, as he moved away from her, back toward his place on the lawn.

For Good

SARAH LAYDEN

Cece is locked inside the rooms of her mind, in the rooms of her parents' house, where they removed the lock and then the whole door. (Long story.) *If you aren't going to keep it open, we'll keep it open for you.* She has been warned. Door open, she can still dream about all the competing hopes buried deep inside her chest. To get a B in algebra. That her parents re-hang her bedroom door and let her live behind it. That she could take back what she said to Juan on last week's sophomore field trip, or that Juan never knew what she said, though she said it loud enough to be heard, on purpose to be heard.

She could not stop thinking about that day at the art museum. They had finished with the Impressionist paintings and the fragile sculptures and the modern art splatters and tiny army men holding up the world, a zillion little figures topped with a Plexiglas platform you could walk on. Looking down, you could see their flat palms held you up. Juan had stomped on the platform—he was forever stomping on things—and the guard wagged a finger, bored, used to the Juans of the world.

So they headed to the gardens on the grounds. A group of them posed with the LOVE sculpture. Robert Indiana was the artist's name, Cece remembered, because how could you forget a name like Robert Indiana? And second, because Juan had made fun of it: Who wants to be named after *this* place? Like saying the word *Indiana* was poison to his mouth. Juan was from Mexico and he never let you forget it. Mexico, where the Coke was sweeter and the soccer was better, where it wasn't even soccer but *fútbol*. He'd been here since sixth grade, but whatever. Mexico this, Mexico that.

"Go back home, then," Cece said, but Juan knew she was joking.

He gripped his heart with one hand. "*Ay de mí*, Cece, wouldn't you miss me? I think you'd miss me even more than I miss Mexico." *Meh-he-co.*

The other boys in the group, a clump of not-Juans, bobbed around her like the taunters they were, when they weren't after your algebra homework (or something else), never-mind that Cece barely passed algebra last quarter. *You still have it bad for Juan, don't you? You think he's The One.*

Not again. Not that again. The One was a stupid game the girls in their class had invented as freshmen. Which boy is The One, the one you're meant to be with? There was a notebook. There is always a notebook. In it were charts and graphs of desirability, with notations like WELL, HE HAS A POOL, or HE WILL WRITE YOU POEMS. Great, if you liked that kind of thing, and Cece guessed she did, although she didn't really know what she liked.

Clarification. She knew *who* she liked, ever since sixth grade, when she and Juan were square dance partners in gym. Ms. Murphy said Juan was a "courtly" dancer, and Juan looked shy for about two seconds before saying, "I know," dancing in that cocky, stompy way, his hand a beautiful feather at her back.

It took her classmates years to adjust to Juan, to stop making fun of his accent and ask him to play basketball. Some never learned to stop ignoring him. Only last year had he grown into his ears and learned how to use his dimples to his advantage. Once he had been Cece's friend alone; now he was best friends with half the school.

For Cece, he was The One. She had marked the notebook with her own hand, swooning in the way girls do when they think they're being private with one another, before they realize there's no such thing. The boys found the notebook. They always do. And every time Cece thought she'd lived down calling Juan SOCCER GOD and HOTTIE OF MEXICAN TELENOVELA PROPORTIONS—she wrote that! She couldn't believe she wrote that!—somebody brought it back up. She would think for five seconds that Juan might share her feelings, and then convince herself otherwise. She'd catch him watching her play soccer, catch him looking at her legs as she ran. Can your legs blush? She felt like her legs were blushing.

Juan never brought up The One. Which was how she knew he was kind, which made her like him more.

Now he was joking at the art museum, always joking, with his brand of like or mock-like. Which was it, and how could you know? The boys were hovering, the girls snickering half-hearted reproaches, *Leave her alone! Jeez*. And Juan came so close that she could smell his soap, which was Dial.

"Cecelia, you're breaking my heart," he sang, in that lilting faded accent that she, in truth, loved.

"Good," she said quickly, surrounded by the sunny blue-sky September day and her pressing friends and her own blood, all forces of heat. "And let me tell you for your own good: it doesn't matter. You. Don't. Matter."

"Ooooh," went the peanut gallery.

Juan's eyes changed, but different from the day Ms. Murphy called him a courtly dancer. His eyes changed to quiet and then they changed into something else, for his own good, for good.

Saturday's Child

KELLY CHERRY

On a morning in May, in 1953, my mother stands at the Formica counter in the kitchen of our house in Charleston, South Carolina, drinking cocoa and smoking a Chesterfield. She wears red lipstick, the only cosmetic she ever bothers with, the shiny tube a staple in her sleek white patent-leather handbag. If it were a weekday she would be getting ready to leave for work in the old Dodge, my father at the wheel, but it is Saturday, and Saturday means laundry, grocery shopping, changing the sheets on the beds. This early in the summer, this early in the morning, and it's already so hot a person could faint. She's wearing a straight linen skirt, dark brown with back kick-pleat, white blouse with a V-neck and batwing sleeves, and brown and white spectator heels, and despite the heat, despite its being Saturday, she wears stockings and a garter belt. She drags on her cigarette, douses it under the faucet. She drops the butt into the ashtray on the kitchen table on her way out. Though the screen door is latched, the back door to the kitchen is left open to let in a breeze, should there be, at some point, a breeze. In the side yard, a parasol of a maple tree spreads a circle of shade. The children use the maple tree as the starting point for games of Hide-and-seek and May I? All day the children chase each other, laugh or cry, climb the monkey bars and swing in the swings. Or they go inside where they read books in their rooms while washing machines make a monotonous chugging sound downstairs. All day the children eat butter-and-sugar sandwiches made with sliced white bread that builds better bodies eight ways. They drink bottle Cokes, the wasp-waist of the bottle fitting neatly in their hands though they do not stop to think about this. They race out again—-letting the screen door slam and bounce, unlatched—-and fling themselves down on the grass, blow milkweed puffs, braiding the ropy stems into bracelets. They practice screaming-in-terror so they can be in the movies. Screaming—-the children have observed that this is what women do most in the movies. Actresses are supposed to be terrorized and scream, then fall backwards onto the bedspread. Playing cowboys and Indians, the children slip Indian-style, as they call it, through the yard, and the maple becomes their tepee. But after a few hours of make-believe they find themselves longing for their own lives, which, after all, are still new to them, unexplored and exciting. And so, though it is Saturday, they play school. They pretend it is a school day and that they are sitting at their small desks, working in workbooks. By mid-afternoon, the neighborhood is as silent as sleep except for the pencils being pushed across the workbooks. These kids know more than they would dream, as yet, of writing. They know that, everywhere they know of, there are expectations and practices with the force of rules. That there's not much difference between the pledge of allegiance and school prayer. People here hold revivals and save themselves. My mother thinks this is pretty idiotic. Pretty, but not completely. Since, she tells herself, the truth is you never know what the score is. But she doesn't tell anyone else that. As far as everyone else is concerned, she's got no use for wishful thinking. This is important to her: she wants everyone to know she has no use for wishful thinking. What she has is a boss who keeps trying to put the make on her. She has a new mortgage—this is the first house she and my father have owned—and she can't afford to lose her job. It's a long day. Saturdays are always long. She chainsmokes. By day's end, the bedrooms have been cleaned, the laundry and groceries put away, the trellis roses pruned and the dogwood trees trimmed, supper served and the dishes washed in the sink and dried by hand. She and my father sit for a while on the back stoop, cicadas and whippoorwills contributing background chatter as if they were guests at a cocktail party, but my parents don't throw parties. Live oaks scrawl shadows on the darkening sky. Magnolia blossoms rustle like silk, brushed by a stirring bird. My mother holds a Coke bottle in one hand, a cigarette in the other. She and my father talk. I don't know what they talk about; their voices are soft, and I am inside, on the other side of the screen door, deeply involved with a biography of Lou Gehrig. The stars come out one by one, like lights turned on in dark houses. Blue deepens into night, and at last there's a breeze. On my face, the air feels like chiffon, billowing like cloth with the sighing breaths of honeysuckle, clover, scented by the dew gathering in droplets on the closed petals of the trellis roses, a perfume that should surely be called Evening in Charleston. My parents' voices are as soft as face powder, as if the South had rubbed all the r's and ending g's down to fine, dissolving outlines. My mother and father come inside and shut the back door. My mother hands the empty Coke bottle to my father and he rinses it out in the sink to keep the ants from being drawn to a sweet residue. There are speck-sized ants that find their way into the cabinets. We keep the lids on jars tightly screwed, the flaps on boxes closed, flour in the refrigerator. My mother crushes her cigarette in the ashtray. All those cigarette butts with red lipstick kissed onto them look like they're bleeding; like tampons. It's like a hemorrhage, that ashtray, like something bursting and flooding.

Hey, Jess McCafferty

CHRISTINE BYL

Hey, Jess McCafferty, what are you doing here? I've never seen you in the store before. I bet you're looking for my sister, but she isn't here, and even if she was, I'd say, "Louisa isn't here right now," because she doesn't love you anyway, Jess. I know you know who I am, but you walk by without saying anything—what's so interesting about the floor? Do you know I'm by myself? Dad trusts me to keep track of things, even though I'm two years younger than Louisa, and besides, she has better things to do than hang around in a hardware store. She says, "You'll understand when you're sixteen, Callie." But I like the smell of the linseed oil Dad rubs into the countertop, and the light in the glass above the front door. I can read when the store's empty. Louisa, she likes things faster than I do. "You can sleep when you're dead," she says.

You think my sister's in love with you, don't you, Jess? I know she's made you think so, sneaking out the window at night, dropping onto the flowers, into your hands. But see, sisters get things about each other, and that's how I know, she's making a fool out of you, Jess. She likes you okay, the way your eyes make her feel, like there's something hot underneath her skin. But like and love are two different things, Jess. "Louisa, you better watch out," I tell her, but she already knows.

You only smile at me because I'm her little sister, otherwise you'd never even see a girl like me, would you? Well, you know what, Jess, Louisa thinks I'm beautiful. She lets me borrow her clothes—I'm wearing her jeans right now, the ones she embroidered at the hem. We wear the same size, but she likes them tight and I like them baggy. "You're so lucky, Callie, you're so skinny," my sister says, and she won't eat at dinner sometimes and she stands in front of the mirror at night and sucks in her cheeks and holds the skin around her middle with both hands. Hey, Jess, did you know that Louisa and I have shared a room since I was born? I could tell my sister from a hundred strangers lying down in the dark just by the way she breathes.

I know how far she lets you go, Jess. Does that shock you? She tells me stuff she doesn't even tell her friends. Never mind what she tells you. I heard her say, "Oh Dad, don't worry, he's definitely *not* my boyfriend." She rolls her eyes and twists her necklaces around her hand so they pinch the skin on her neck. If I told you that right now, Jess, you'd drop your eyes and smile and you'd act like you didn't care, but if my sister didn't love you and you knew it, you'd care.

Anyway, Louisa is smarter than you think. Sometimes she lies on the bed on her back and she traces the outline of herself. She presses her finger into the top of her head, runs it along her hair, down over her ear, under her chin where it meets her neck and all the way down until she can't reach without bending and then she starts up the other side. Let me tell you, Jess, Louisa knows where she starts and where she ends.

What are you up to, Jess, running those hands over everything? Don't you know what you're looking for? I bet it's not a socket set. I'm not going to ask you if you need any help. If you need it, you can ask. Do you even know my name? I think you do, even though I know Louisa doesn't talk about me when you guys park in your junky pickup, or lie out in the back field with your hands up her shirt. I've watched you, Jess, the way you jog alongside her in the dark as she tilts her head away. In the morning, I can see the places where your feet pressed down in the wet grass, and she tells me where you went and what you did anyway, so you've got no secrets from me, Jess McCafferty.

Are you still watching to see if she's going to come out from the curtain behind the register? Are you looking at me? You think I don't see you because I'm reading, but if you were close, you'd see it's just a catalog for lawn tools. You're used to the feel of eyes on you, anyway, aren't you, Jess, all the girls in three grades crazy about you, something about your tan arms and faded shirts and the way your bones fit under the skin of your face.

But come on, Jess, you can see she isn't here so you might as well leave because you are starting to look aimless, and I don't think that's how you want to look. My dad will be back any minute, and he'll say something to you, you can bet on it. Is this how you first looked at Louisa, quick meeting her eyes, then smiling after you look away? You can't love her like she needs to be loved, Jess McCafferty. She's too much for you, and deep down, you already know it. You need a simpler kind of girl and I'm not saying she's me, but just think twice about Louisa.

Hey, Jess McCafferty, you think I can't see you over there? I saw you slip that in your pocket, looking at me between the shelves. Who do you think you are? It doesn't matter what I say, does it, Jess. I can't change how you feel about Louisa. But I could get you in such trouble, I could tell my father just like that, you know. I'd do it, too, watch me. Hey Dad, I'd say, Jess McCafferty was around here today, looking for Louisa, taking what isn't his.

The Two Rats and the BB Gun

RAPHAEL DAGOLD

Two rats were biding their time in an alley by a small pile of garbage, waiting for a boy with a BB gun to go in for dinner.

"Listen," one of the rats said to the other, "we'll be waiting here forever for that kid to go in. His mother's a drunk and is probably passed out on the couch. Let's make a run for it together. He'll be confused, and we know his aim is bad."

As the first rat made its dash, the second stayed behind to see how he fared. At that moment, the boy's mother called out:

"You come in here with that BB gun before I have to come out and get you."

Rolling his eyes, the boy didn't see the first rat cross to safety. The second, seeing his friend pass without a shot, walked confidently into the open. The boy, having stayed to spite his mother, took a last shot, his most careful of the evening.

Sometimes, chance intervenes where plans fail.

About the Authors

STEVE ALMOND is the author of the story collections *My Life in Heavy Metal, God Bless America,* and *The Evil B. B. Chow;* the novel *Which Brings Me to You* (with Julianna Baggott); and the nonfiction books *Candyfreak, (Not That You Asked)* and *Rock and Roll Will Save Your Life.* He lives in Arlington, Massachusetts.

BETH ALVARADO'S story collection, *Not a Matter of Love,* won the Many Voices Prize. She teaches at the University of Arizona, Tucson.

JON ANDERSEN teaches English at Quinebaug Valley Community College in Danielson and Willimantic, Connecticut, and is the author of a book of poems, *Stomp and Sing,* and the editor of the anthology, *Seeds of Fire: Contemporary Poetry from the Other U. S. A.*

ANN ANGEL is the author of the young adult biography *Janis Joplin, Rise up Singing* and was contributing editor of the highly acclaimed *Such a Pretty Face: Short Stories about Beauty.* Angel teaches writing at Mount Mary College, Milwaukee, Wisconsin, she now lives in Brooklyn, New York.

PETER BACHO is the author of six books, including *Cebu,* which won the American Book Award in 1992, and most recently, *Leaving Yesler.* He is a foremost chronicler of the Filipino-American experience. He lives in Tacoma, Washington, and teaches at Evergreen State College.

RICHARD BAUSCH is the author of eleven novels (including *Hello to the Cannibals* and *Peace*) and eight collections of short stories (*Something Is Out There* and *The Stories of Richard Bausch*). His stories have appeared in *The Atlantic, Esquire, Harper's, The New Yorker, The Southern Review, The Best American Short Stories, The O. Henry Prize Stories,* and elsewhere. Among his many awards are a Guggenheim Fellowship, an award from the American Academy of Arts and Letters, and the 2004 PEN/Malamud Award for Excellence in the Short Story. He is on the faculty of the writing program at the University of Memphis.

DAPHNE BEAL is the author of the novel In the *Land of No Right Angles.* Her fiction has appeared in *Open City* and *The Mississippi Review* and is anthologized in T*he KGB Bar Reader.* She has published essays in *McSweeney's, The New York Times Magazine,* and most recently, in the collection, *Freud's Blind Spot: 23 Original Essays on Siblings.* Beal teaches creative writing at New York University and lives in Brooklyn.

DANIEL LEVIN BECKER is a writer, critic, translator, font enthusiast, and the youngest member of the Paris-based literary collective, Oulipo. He lives in San Francisco.

BRIAN BEDARD directs the creative writing program of the University of South Dakota, is the editor of *South Dakota Review* and the author of two story collections, including *Grieving on the Run,* which won the Serena McDonald Kennedy Fiction Award and was nominated for the 2008 National Book Award.

GAYLE BRANDEIS's most recent publications are the novel *Delta Girls* and a novel for young adults, *My Life with the Lincolns*. Her first novel, *The Book of Dead Birds*, won the Bellwether Prize. She lives in Riverside, California.

RICHARD BRAUTIGAN (d. 1984) was a novelist, poet, and short story writer best known for his novel *Trout Fishing in America* (1967). Among his other works of fiction are *In Watermelon Sugar, The Revenge of the Lawn*, and *A Confederate General from Big Sur*.

CHRISTINE BYL lives in Healy, Alaska. "Hey, Jess McCafferty" is from a collection in progress, *Deep Enough for Drowning*. Her prose has been published in *Glimmer Train, Bellingham Review, The Sun, Lumberyard*, and several anthologies.

DONALD CAPONE's stories have appeared in *Edgar Literary Magazine, Word Riot*, Weekly Reader's READ magazine, and *Thieves Jargon*, as well as in the anthologies *See You Next Tuesday, Skive Quarterly 6, The Ampersand, Ten Best Stories of 2010*, and *Rebellion: New Voices of Fiction*. He is the author of the comic novel *Into the Sunset*.

ALAN STEWART CARL is a writer of fiction and miscellany. His work has been published in *Hayden's Ferry Review, Mid-American Review, PANK, Monkeybicycle*, and elsewhere. He is currently at work on a novel and stories. He lives in San Antonio, Texas.

RON CARLSON is the author of ten books of fiction, including the novels *The Signal* and *Five Skies*, which was selected as a best book of 2007 by the *Los Angeles Times* and as the One Book Rhode Island in 2009. His stories have been published in *The New Yorker, Harper's*, and *Esquire*, and anthologized in *Best American Short Stories, The O. Henry Prize Stories*, and

The Norton Anthology of Short Fiction. He is on the faculty of the University of California, Irvine.

KELLY CHERRY is the author of nineteen books of poetry, fiction, and nonfiction. Her work has been widely published in quarterlies and selected for inclusion in prize anthologies: *Best American Short Stories, The O. Henry Prize Stories, The Pushcart Prize,* and *New Stories from the South.* Among her books are *The Exiled Heart: A Meditative Autobiography, Girl in a Library: On Women Writers and the Writing Life,* and *The Society of Friends: Stories.* Cherry lives in Halifax, Virginia.

RAPHAEL DAGOLD has published poetry and prose in *Quarterly West, Frank, Indiana Review, Northwest Review, Washington Square,* and elsewhere. He has taught writing at Lewis and Clark College, and is pursuing a doctorate in writing and literature at the University of Utah. He lives in Salt Lake City.

AZIZAT DANMOLE lives in St. Louis, Missouri, where she is a private editor for ESL students. She is also pursuing a new interest in poetry. "Between Practice and Perfection" is her first publication.

SAMANTHA DAVIS grew up in Massachusetts, and currently lives on Douglas Island, in Alaska. She teaches eighth grade English, and is an MFA student in the University of Alaska Anchorage's low-residency program. She is at work on a young adult novel.

STUART DYBEK is the author of three books of fiction, *I Sailed With Magellan, The Coast of Chicago* (a One Book One Chicago selection), and *Childhood and Other Neighborhoods,* and two collections of poetry, *Streets in Their Own Ink* and *Brass Knuckles.* His work has been published in *The New*

Yorker, Harper's, The Atlantic, Poetry, Tin House, and many other magazines, and has been widely anthologized. He is writer-in-residence at Northwestern University.

DAVE EGGERS is the author of seven books including *Zeitoun, What Is the What,* and *A Heartbreaking Work of Staggering Genius.* He is the founder and editor of *McSweeney's,* an independent publishing house based in San Francisco. In 2002, with Ninive Calegari, he co-founded 826 Valencia, a nonprofit writing and tutoring center for youth in the Mission District of San Francisco. Eggers is a native of Chicago, and now lives in the San Francisco Bay area.

PIA Z. EHRHARDT is the author of *Famous Fathers & Other Stories.* Her stories and essays have appeared in *McSweeney's Quarterly Concern, Oxford American,* and *Narrative Magazine.* They have also been featured on NPR's *Selected Shorts,* and widely anthologized. Ehrhardt is writer-in-residence at the New Orleans Center for Creative Arts. She lives in New Orleans.

ELIZABETH EHRLICH is the author of *Miriam's Kitchen: A Memoir,* winner of a National Jewish Book Award and selected as a New York Times Notable Book. She lives in Westchester County, New York.

ERIN FANNING is the author of *The Curse of Blackhawk Bay* and *Mountain Biking Michigan,* as well as numerous short stories, essays, and articles. She lives in northern Michigan.

L.C. FIORE is the author of a novel, *Green Gospel,* and has published stories in *Folio, MAKE Magazine, Michigan Quarterly Review,* and *Wascana Review,* among others. An award-winning short story writer and editor, his work has also appeared on NPR and in various baseball annuals. He divides his time between Chicago, Illinois, and Durham, North Carolina.

JENNY HALPER's fiction has appeared in *Wigleaf Top 50 Very Short Stories 2009, SmokeLong Quarterly, Frigg,* and *New English Fiction Meetinghouse.* She recently co-wrote a script with Susan Seidelman and adapted a novel for Pretty Pictures. At the New York independent film company Mandalay Vision, she has worked on many films including Lisa Choledenko's *The Kids Are All Right* and *The Whistleblower.* She lives in New York City.

AARON HAMBURGER has published a novel, *Faith for Beginners,* and a story collection, *The View from Stalin's Head,* as well as short pieces in *Tin House, Details, Boulevard,* and elsewhere. He teaches at Columbia and New York University and lives in New York City.

TOM HAZUKA has published three novels, *The Road to the Island, In the City of the Disappeared,* and *Last Chance for First,* as well as a book of nonfiction, *A Method to March Madness: An Insider's Look at the Final Four* (co-written with C. J. Jones). He is a co-editor of the present anthology, *Sudden Flash Youth,* and of three others, *Flash Fiction, You Have Time for This,* and *A Celestial Omnibus: Short Fiction on Faith.* He teaches fiction writing at Central Connecticut State University.

JIM HEYNEN's short-shorts and prose poems featuring young farm boys appear in his collections—*The One Room Schoolhouse, The Boys' House, You Know What Is Right,* and *The Man Who Kept Cigars in His Cap.* Also among his many other publications are two young adult novels, *Cosmos Coyote and William the Nice* and *Being Youngest,* and a nonfiction book, *One Hundred Over 100,* which features one hunded American centenarians. He lives in St. Paul, Minnesota.

MATT HLINAK is on the faculty of The School of Continuing Studies at Northwestern University, where he teaches courses in English and law. His creative works have recently appeared in *Post*, *The Mayo Review*, *Midwest Literary Magazine*, *Review Americana*, and *NewCity Chicago*. He lives in Chicago.

MEG KEARNEY's most recent collection of poetry, *Home By Now*, won the 2010 L. L. Winship / PEN New England Award. She is the author of *The Secret of Me*, a novel-in-verse about being an adopted child, and a sequel, *The Girl in the Mirror*. Kearney is the director of the Solstice Creative Writing Programs of Pine Manor College in Chestnut Hill, Massachusetts. She lives in New Ipswich, New Hampshire.

JACQUELINE KOLOSOV's young adult novels include *The Red Queen's Daughter*, *A Sweet Disorder*, and *Grace from China*. Her second poetry collection, *Modigliani's Muse*, is a biography in poems that looks at the artist and his circle of friends and lovers. She lives in Lubbeck, Texas.

BILL KONIGSBERG is an award-winning sports writer for the Associated Press and ESPN.com and the author of two novels, *Out of the Pocket*, winner of a 2009 Lambda Literary award, and *Openly Straight* (2012). His essay "Sports World Still a Struggle for Gays" won a GLAAD Media Award for Outstanding Digital Journalism. Konigsberg teaches writing at Arizona State University.

MATT KRAMPITZ lives and works in Bristol, Connecticut. He teaches English at Lewis Mills High School. "Half Sleep" is his first published short story.

SARAH LAYDEN's short fiction can be found in *Stone Canoe*, *Artful Dodge*, *The Evansville Review*, *Zone 3*, *PANK*, *Wigleaf*, and elsewhere. She also writes poems and has published a novel, *Sleeping Woman*. She teaches writing at Indiana

University-Purdue University and Marian University, both in Indianapolis.

CARON A. LEVIS was born and raised in New York City, where she now works as a teaching artist, using drama to teach self-awareness, communication, and conflict resolution in schools. She has published fiction in *Fence,* and in 2010, her short play, *Flight Risk,* was selected for Manhattan Theatre Source's EstroGenius Festival.

PAUL LISICKY is the author of the novels *Lawnboy* and *The Burning House,* and of the memoir, *Famous Builder.* He currently teaches at New York University and lives in New York City and Springs, New York. His most recent work is *Unbuilt Projects,* a collection of short prose pieces.

DAVID LLOYD directs the Creative Writing Program at Le Moyne College in Syracuse, New York. Among his books are *The Urgency of Identity: Contemporary English-Language Poetry from Wales, The Everyday Apocalypse, Boys: Stories and a Novella,* and a new, expanded edition of his poetry collection *The Gospel According to Frank.*

ANNE MAZER is the award-winning author of more than forty books for young readers, including the classic picture book *The Salamander Room,* novels such as *The Oxboy,* and the bestselling *The Amazing Days of Abby Hayes* series and the *Sister Magic* series. Her latest work, *Spilling Ink: A Handbook for Young Writers,* was co-authored with Ellen Potter. Mazer lives in Ithaca, New York.

NAOMI SHIHAB NYE is the author of numerous books of poetry and prose, including the poetry collections *Red Suitcase, Fuel,* and *You & Yours; Never in a Hurry,* essays; and *Habibi,* a young adult novel. She edited the anthologies *19*

Varieties of Gazelle: Poems of the Middle East, This Same Sky: A Collection of Poems from Around the World, and others. Nye lives in San Antonio, Texas.

KATHLEEN O'DONNELL is a copywriter who has written for J. Crew, Bloomingdale's, and Saks Fifth Avenue, among others. She is currently at work on an interactive romance for young adults. She lives in New York City. "First Virtual" is her first published story.

MARYANNE O'HARA is a longtime editor at *Ploughshares* and the author of many short stories, the most recent of which have appeared in *The North American Review, Five Points,* and the anthology *The Art of Friction.* A novel, *The End of September,* is nearly complete. She lives near Boston.

PAMELA PAINTER's story collections are *Getting to Know the Weather, The Long and Short of It,* and *Wouldn't You Like to Know.* She is co-author of *What If? Writing Exercises for Fiction Writers.* Her stories have appeared in *The Atlantic, Harper's, Kenyon Review, Ploughshares, Quick Fiction,* and elsewhere. Painter teaches creative writing at Emerson College, Boston.

JONATHAN PAPERNICK is the author of *The Ascent of Eli Israel; Who by Fire, Who by Blood;* and *There Is No Other.* He teaches fiction writing at Emerson College and in the BIMA program at Brandeis University.

DAVID PARTENHEIMER is on the faculty of Truman State University in Kirksville, Missouri, where he lives. He has published scholarly articles, translations, and creative works. "Pep Assembly at Evergreen Junior High" is his first published short story.

TODD JAMES PIERCE is the author of five books and anthologies, including *Newsworld,* which won the Drue

Heinz Literature Prize. His work has been published widely in periodicals, including *The Georgia Review, The Gettysburg Review, The Iowa Review, The Missouri Review,* and *North American Review.* He teaches at California Polytechnic State University and lives in Santa Barbara County.

SONIA PILCER is the author of five novels, including *Teen Angel, Maiden Rites, Little Darlings, I-Land: Manhattan in Monologue,* and *The Holocaust Kid,* which was adapted as a theatrical play. She teaches at the Writers Voice in Manhattan, and at Berkshire Community College in Great Barrington, Massachusetts. She lives in Hillsdale, New York.

SHELBY RAEBECK lives in East Hampton, New York, where he teaches at the Ross School and coaches sports. He has published short stories in the *Mid-American Review, Callaloo,* and elsewhere, and is currently working on two novels.

ERIKA RECORDON is at work on her first collection of stories. Her fiction has appeared in *the journal, Poor Claudia, The Denver Quarterly,* and in online publications. She lives in Portland, Oregon, and works at a fancy grocery store.

BRUCE HOLLAND ROGERS has won the Nebula Award, the World Fantasy Award, and the Pushcart Prize for his stories. He teaches at the Northwest Institute for Literary Arts in Freeland, Washington. His home base is Eugene, Oregon.

ROBERT SHAPARD co-edits the sudden fiction anthologies for W. W. Norton. The latest is *Sudden Fiction Latino: Short-Short Stories from the United States and Latin America.* He also co-edited *Flash Fiction Forward.* A chapbook of his own short-shorts, *Motel and Other Stories,* was published in 2005. He lives in Austin, Texas.

MANUELA SOARES is on the faculty of Pace University's MS

in Publishing Program. Among her books are *The Joy Within: A Beginner's Guide to Meditation* (with Joan Goldstein), *One Hand Clapping: Zen Stories for All Ages* (with Rafe Martin), *Butch/Femme,* and *ESP McGee and the Dolphin's Message* (pseudonym Jesse Rodgers). She lives in New York City.

CRAIG MORGAN TEICHER's books are *Brenda Is in the Room and Other Poems* and *Cradle Book.* He works as an editor at *Publishers Weekly* magazine and teaches creative writing at various universities in New York City.

NATALIE HANEY TILGHMAN is a graduate student in creative writing at Pacific Lutheran University. Her work has appeared in *Crab Creek Review, Santa Clara Review, South Loop Review,* and in *Dots on a Map,* a fiction anthology. Tilghman was a Visiting Artist at the American Academy in Rome in 2010. She lives in Chicago.

ALISON TOWNSEND is the author of several books of poetry, including *Persephone in America, The Blue Dress,* and *What the Body Knows.* Her poems and creative nonfiction have appeared in *Crab Orchard Review, Rattle,* and *Southern Review,* among others. She teaches at the University of Wisconsin-Whitewater and lives in the farm country outside Madison.

NANCE VAN WINCKEL has published five collections of poems and three collections of short fiction. She recently received a Christopher Isherwood Fiction Fellowship, and new short fiction can be found in *AGNI, The Massachusetts Review,* and *Kenyon Review.* She teaches writing at the Vermont College of Fine Arts.

THOMAS JEFFREY VASSEUR is the author of *Discovering the World: Thirteen Stories* and *Touch the Earth: An Aftermath of the Vietnam War.* He has received a Utah Fiction Award, an NEH Grant to UC Berkeley, and is a two-time finalist for Georgia's Townsend Award for fiction. He lives in Valdosta, Georgia, and is a professor at Valdosta State University.

HANNAH BOTTOMY VOSKUIL's work has appeared in several anthologies including the *The Seagull Reader, 2nd. Ed.*, and *Flash Fiction Forward.* Voskuil's short stories have appeared in literary magazines such as *Quarterly West, South Dakota Review,* and *The South Carolina Review.* She lives in Somerville, Massachusetts.

ALICE WALKER is the author of several novels, including *By the Light of My Father's Smile, The Temple of My Familiar,* and *The Color Purple* (winner of the Pulitzer Prize and the National Book Award), as well as many celebrated collections of short stories, poems and essays.

BRYAN SHAWN WANG has published flash fiction in *Vestal Review* and *flashquake,* and has been nominated for a Pushcart Prize. He is working on a novel for children and a collection of stories for adults. Wang lives in Wyomissing, Pennsylvania.

MILES GARETT WATSON's work has appeared in *Quarterly West, River Styx, Poetry,* and *The Oxford American.* He lives in Searcy, Arkansas, and teaches at Arkansas State University and Searcy High School, where he also coaches baseball.

KATHARINE WEBER is the author of the novels *True Confection, Triangle, The Little Women, The Music Lesson,* and *Objects in Mirror Are Closer Than They Appear.* Her short fiction has appeared in *The New Yorker, Story, Southwest Review, Vestal Review,* and elsewhere. She lives in Bethany, Connecticut.

LEX WILLIFORD has taught in the writing programs at Southern Illinois University, the University of Missouri, and the University of Alabama. His book, *Macauley's Thumb,* won the 1993 Iowa Short Fiction Award. Co-editor of the *Scribner Anthology of Contemporary Short Fiction* and the *Touchstone Anthology of Contemporary Nonfiction,* he directs the online MFA at the University of Texas, El Paso.

LEIGH ALLISON WILSON is the author of the short story collections *From the Bottom Up* (winner of the Flannery O'Connor Award) and *Wind.* Her work has appeared in *Harper's, Mademoiselle, The Kenyon Review, The Southern Review, Grand Stree*t, and elsewhere. She lives in Oswego, New York, on Lake Ontario.

SHOLEH WOLPÉ is the author of two books of poetry, *Rooftops of Tehran* and *The Scar Saloon,* and the translator of *Sin: Selected Poems of Forugh Farrokhzad.* She is a regional editor of *Tablet & Pen: Literary Landscapes from the Modern Middle East* and poetry editor of the *Levantine Review,* an online journal about the Middle East. Her poems, translations, essays, stories, and reviews have appeared in scores of literary journals and anthologies worldwide. Wolpé was born in Iran and presently lives in Los Angeles.

About the Editors

MARK BUDMAN's fiction and nonfiction have appeared in *The Mississippi Review, Virginia Quarterly, The London Magazine, McSweeney's, Sonora Review, Southeast Review, Mid-American Review,* and in the anthology *Flash Fiction Forward.* He is the author of a novel, *My Life at First Try,* co-editor of *You Have Time for This* and *Best American Flash Fiction of the 21st Century,* and publisher of the flash fiction magazine *Vestal Review.* He lives in Vestal, New York.

TOM HAZUKA has published three novels, *The Road to the Island, In the City of the Disappeared,* and *Last Chance for First,* as well as a nonfiction work, *A Method to March Madness: An Insider's Look at the Final Four* (co-written with C. J. Jones). He has co-edited the anthologies *Flash Fiction, You Have Time for This, A Celestial Omnibus: Short Fiction on Faith,* and *Best American Flash Fiction of the 21st Century.* He teaches fiction writing at Central Connecticut State University. He lives in Berlin, Connecticut.

CHRISTINE PERKINS-HAZUKA has taught in both private and public middle and high schools for thirty years. The high school creative writing course she developed and taught spurred her interest in collecting short-short stories of particular interest to students. She lives in Berlin, Connecticut.

Acknowledgments

"Stop," by Steve Almond. Copyright © 2003, 2011 by Steve Almond. First published in somewhat different form in *The Sun*. Reprinted by permission of the author. All rights reserved.

"History," by Beth Alvarado. Copyright © 2011 by Beth Alvarado. Published by arrangement with the author. All rights reserved.

"The Call," by Jon Andersen. Copyright © 2011 by Jon Andersen. Published by arrangement with the author. All rights reserved.

"The Bracelet," by Ann Angel. Copyright © 2009 by Ann Angel. Published by arrangement with the author. All rights reserved.

"Beyond Yesler," by Peter Bacho. Copyright © 2010 by Peter Bacho. First published in somewhat different form in the novel *Leaving Yesler*. Reprinted by permission of the author. All rights reserved.

"1951," by Richard Bausch. From *Someone to Watch Over Me*. Copyright © 1999 by Richard Bausch. Reprinted by permission of HarperCollins Publishers, New York.

"Heartland," by Daphne Beal. Copyright © 2011 by Daphne Beal. Published by arrangement with the author. All rights reserved.

"The Perpetual Now," by Daniel Levin Becker. Copyright © 2011 by Daniel Levin Becker. Published by arrangement with the author. All rights reserved.

"Coyote Bait," by Brian Bedard. Copyright © 2000 by Brian Bedard. First published in *South Dakota Review* (Vol. 38, No. 3). Reprinted by permission of the author. All rights reserved.

"Rapture," by Gayle Brandeis. Copyright © 2004 by Gayle Brandeis. First published in a slightly different form in *Vestal Review*. Published here by arrangement with the author. All rights reserved.

"Corporal," by Richard Brautigan. From *Revenge of the Law, the Abortion,*